He Loves Me,
He Loves You Not 4

Avionne's Return

A Novel

MYCHEA

Good2Go Publishing

ISBN: 9780990869498

Copyright ©2015 by Mychea

Published 2015 by Good2Go Publishing

7311 W. Glass Lane • Laveen, AZ 85339

www.good2gopublishing.com

twitter @good2gobooks

G2G@good2gopublishing.com

Facebook.com/good2gopublishing

ThirdLane Marketing: Brian James

Brian@good2gopublishing.com

Cover design: Davida Baldwin

Books by This Author

Coveted

Vengeance

He Loves Me, He Loves You Not

He Loves Me, He Loves You Not 2

He Loves Me, He Loves You Not 3

He Loves Me, He Loves You Not 4

My Boyfriend's Wife

DVD

Stage Play of My Boyfriend's Wife

Acknowledgments

This is my seventh novel and I want to take the time to thank all of the individuals that helped to bring it into existence. I would first like to start by thanking God for giving me the gift of a vivid imagination and creative writing. I also want to thank my family and extended family for their continued support throughout the years.

Marcy Patrick what can I really say ... thank you for just being there. You are one of the ones that has been down since my very first manuscript. Nothing can compare to everything you have been to me for the last million years of our lives. And I love you to death. Thank you.

Nikki G. Jackson, my sister from another. Love you to the moon and back for always. You are truly irreplaceable.

Me'Shell Stewart, girl there are not enough words! Lol! But you already know. Love you till the death of me...can y'all believe we've known each other since we were five?!! LOL!

Marcie Rodriquez, my LL. You rock. Love you to pieces!! Thank you for being such an amazing friend. Couldn't imagine life without your feistiness. LOL! (I'm just saying.)

Last but definitely not least, I want to thank you the readers. Thank you for being there since my very first book Coveted and holding me down until now. There will never be enough ways and enough days to express how much I value you. Now it's time to let the fun begin! Enjoy!

Email: mychea@mychea.com

Website: www.mychea.com

He Loves Me, He Loves You Not 4

Avionne's Return

RECAP

**HE LOVES ME
HE LOVES YOU NOT 3**

Elliott was seeing red as he waited for Shayla who was now exiting the Marriott. "This is what you have been doing with your time? Who was that man?" he blurted out as soon as he saw her.

Phylicia narrowed her eyes, surprised to see Elliott standing by her car in the parking lot, "You followed me?"

"You bet your life I followed you," he said harshly. "You've been all secretive. Did you think I wouldn't be curious as to where my woman was heading at all hours of the night?"

Phylicia felt sad for Elliott. She could care less about what he was speaking of as she said a mini prayer for his soul in her head.

"Why did you leave your daughter with that man?"

Phylicia shrugged. "That's none of your business," she said, as she attempted to push past him so that she could gain access to her car.

Elliott pushed her back, catching her off guard, causing her to fall backwards onto the pavement.

Phylicia was shell-shocked as she sat on the ground, staring up at Elliott, observing him in a new light.

"You think I don't know who you are, Shayla? Better yet Phylicia?" Elliott gave her a pointed look, "I make it my business to know everyone that I deal with."

Phylicia began clapping very disrespectfully from her sitting position. She was angry with herself for allowing this to happen. She was slippin' and clearly losing her touch. *The old Phylicia never would have allowed anyone to catch her off guard like this,* she thought. It was definitely time to hang it up. Any good thing ending needed a last hurrah and a last hurrah she was going to have.

"So you do a little research and you think you've got me all figured out now? Is that what it is?" Phylicia asked him incredulously as she pushed herself up to a standing position not wanting to bring any unwanted attention their way.

"Don't I?" Elliott asked.

Phylicia shrugged, "You tell me. You're the one over here spitting knowledge ... maybe I'll learn something as you continue talking." She told him sarcastically.

Elliott raised his hand and slapped Phylicia across her face. No one spoke to him in such a manner and got away with it. She wasn't going to be the first.

Phylicia touched her tongue to her lip, tasting the blood where she felt a small cut from where Elliott had hit her. Her temper wanted to flare up, but she didn't allow it. He wanted to feel as if he was in the power position and she wanted that for him.

"Do you feel better now?" she asked him. "Can we please go back to the house and not fight in a parking lot?"

Elliott eyed her skeptically. He'd done his research. He wasn't afraid of her, but he also knew that she couldn't be trusted.

"We can finish this discussion at home if that will make you more comfortable."

"Thank you. I don't want to cause a scene here and would feel more comfortable at home."

Phylicia took her key lock out of her pocket and unlocked her car as Elliott opened the door for her to get in. Once she was inside and he closed her car door, she sped off without giving her car a moment's time to warm up.

****

Arriving at the house considerably sooner than Elliott, Phylicia quickly began removing the bulbs from each light fixture in the house, as well as making sure that every door and window in the house was locked. Acting quickly, she went to the hall closet and plugged each iron she owned into a wall socket, giving them time to heat up. Pulling her long hair into a ponytail, she moved every knife she owned in the kitchen out from the cabinet drawer and dropped them into the laundry basket in the basement. All pots and pans were placed inside the washing machine. Phylicia was on her way to grab some rope when she heard Elliott's truck pull into the driveway.

Walking slowly to a window at the side of the house, she watched as he exited his truck at a snail's pace and moved his head from side to side, seemingly trying to take in his surroundings.

Phylicia smirked as he made his way in through the front door. *What an amateur*, she thought, as she waited for the front door to open.

After a few minutes with no motion, her head snapped towards the den when she heard what sounded like a window resisting a push. Remaining in her location, Phylicia stayed crouched within the shadows. She never went towards danger, danger had to come to her, and from there they would duke it out. Breathing in and out slowly as to not make much noise, she forced her hearing sense to pick up. Turning her head to the right, she heard a noise in the bathroom; she listened as the glass broke.

Phylicia knew better though. The glass breaking was a decoy. Elliott had no intention of coming in through the miniature bathroom window. His plan was to get her to go in there to trap her, but Phylicia knew better. She laughed silently to herself; he was dealing with a professional. *His body count probably hasn't even hit ten yet*, she thought to herself, and he thought that he was ready to take her on. She was excited, as it had been a long time since she was in a game of cat and mouse, and she had the patience to play all night.

After a full ten minutes passed with no action or sound, Phylicia smiled when she heard faint footsteps on the stairs coming from the basement. *Bout time*, she thought. *Let the games begin!* The door to the basement creaked open and then stopped. If Phylicia weren't playing this game of life with him, she would have laughed. *Oh Elliott*, she thought, unhooking a knife from her ankle clip and threw it across the room.

"Ahhhh," Elliott yelled out. Glancing down, he realized that a knife had struck him in his left side. Clutching his side, he quickly pulled the knife out before it did any more damage. Blood continued to ooze out of the spot.

Phylicia smiled when she hit her target. *Assassins 101: know how to be a knife thrower*, she thought. He was pathetic. *What did I ever see in him?* she thought to herself.

"You Bitch!" Elliott screamed in pain, as he staggered around by the stairs.

Saying nothing, Phylicia pulled another knife from her ankle clip. Aiming at his neck this time, she flicked her wrist and let the knife sail through the air.

"Ahhhhhhhhhhhhhhhhhhhhhhh," Elliott yelled as he tried to grab his neck, but losing his balance in the process and falling back down the basement stairs.

Phylicia ran to the steps as swift as a ninja. Gazing down the staircase to see Elliott withering in

16

pain, she shook her head, "First guy I date in over a decade and I choose a wimp." Pulling another knife out of her ankle clip, she watched him for a minute before aiming the knife directly at his face. She was pleased when his withering stopped and he was now reduced to only moaning. Walking down the stairs as graceful as a swan, Phylicia stood over Elliott, who had a gash oozing blood in his side, a knife stuck in his chest and the last knife Phylicia had thrown protruding out of one of his eye sockets, he was a sight for sore eyes.

Standing over top of him as he continued to moan, Phylicia straddled him and knelt down so that she could sit on his chest, which meant also sitting on the knife that with the extra force went directly through his heart.

Jerking as the knife went through his body, Elliott's one good eye tried to focus on Phylicia's face, illuminated only by the glimpses of light through the blinds from the streetlights. "Why?"

"Because you did not know your place. Look at you now as you struggle to breathe." She crossed her arms and leaned down staring into his one good eye. "You started a war you weren't equipped to win." Phylicia watched as his breathing became more and more ragged before she felt his heart pump no more. Eyeing one of the irons that she had plugged in she retrieved it and brought it over to Elliott. Even though he was dead, she couldn't resist holding the hot iron to his skin and smiling as his flesh began to burn.

I'm hungry, Phylicia realized as she stood up, unplugging the iron and bouncing up the basement stairs, leaving Elliott to rot in his own blood. Tacos are just what the doctor ordered she thought as she entered the kitchen to begin thawing out ground beef on the stove, in preparation for her dinner.

****

Shia groggily answered her cell. She stayed in Trent's hotel room late again the previous night and her body was reminding her quite effectively that she wasn't the young spring chicken that she used to be and that these late night on the creep sex sessions she was having with her husband was not helping. They decided that Trent would spend a few more nights at the hotel so that they could try to put the spice back into their relationship. The sex was good, the not getting much sleep was the part she was having a rough time with and was not the business.

"Good Morning," she whispered into the phone.

"Mmm, sounds like a goodnight from over here." A low deep voice laughed.

"Baby." Shia half cried, half groaned. "Why are you calling me so early?"

Trent smirked into the phone, "You're going to regret that statement once you hear what I have to say and you will be very grateful about what I have to say to you."

"I'll be the judge of that." Shia croaked as she lay with her eyes closed waiting to hear what he had to say."

"You're *so* gonna owe me." Trent said continuing to play.

"Oh my God Trent, what do you want? Did you just call to wake me up to play on my phone?" Shia laughed tiredly.

"Okay, okay, okay your highness. No, I did not just call to wake you up or play on your phone, but either way I wanted to hear your voice."

Shia remained quiet waiting for her husband to get to the point refusing to entertain him any longer.

Trent got the hint through her silence, "I have a little present for you."

"You are my present. What can be greater than you?" Shia commented.

Trent smiled, "You're my gift every day of my life to babe, but this present is amazing. This is the second time that I get to announce to you this package has ten fingers and ten toes and we will call her Luna. She's a little heavier this go round though."

Shia's eyes sprang open and she quickly sat up on the bed. "What? What do you mean?"

"I mean, right here in my arms is a little bundle of joy that calls me daddy and what do you call her?" he asked someone in the background.

"Mommy!" A chipper voice came across Shia's airwaves.

"Luna! My baby, oh my gosh! Are you okay?"

"Yes, Mommy. Daddy got me some ice cream."

Shia tried to laugh, but was too choked up with emotion, "Did he? Is it good?"

"Yes. I miss you Mommy."

Shia closed her eyes and held the phone so close to her face that they may as well have been fused together. "I miss you to, punkin. I love you."

"Love you too Mommy."

"I have her babe, she's safe. We're on the way to the house now." Trent said into the receiver reclaiming control of his cell.

"This is crazy! I am so glad you called me this morning. I apologize for giving you such a hard time."

"I didn't take it personally. I'm used to you." Trent laughed, "We'll be there in about five minutes. So up and at 'em."

"You're so silly. Okay, see you two in a few." Shia said, hanging up the phone.

****

As the door opened, Shia was in a state of shock. She couldn't believe what was happening. Tears began streaming down her face so hard that she had to keep blinking-fixing her blurry vision. There in her doorway was her estranged husband holding a baby girl, her baby girl Luna had finally made her way home.

"Mommy!"

"Oh my God." Shia exclaimed as Luna leapt into her arms. "My baby has returned home. Thank you, God. Thank you, God," she said wiping her eyes as she held the toddler tightly refusing to let Luna go. "Prayer changes everything. I knew in my heart that my baby would come back to us. I knew it."

Luna's eyes were closed as she held onto her mother. Tears also escaped the little girls face. Shia was beside herself. Her baby's kidnapping had consumed her. Now she just wanted to hold her and never let her go again. She was still finding it hard to believe that she was home again. Her baby girl was here in her arms, it all seemed so surreal to her.

"Hey baby, how was your day?" Trent asked entering their house, waving at Shia trying to get her attention. "Doesn't the delivery boy get a kiss, or do they all go to the found princess?"

"I'm so sorry!" Shia said leaning up to kiss Trent as he bent down to her, she hadn't meant to be dismissive of him. She was just bursting with excitement.

"Luna is like, right here!" she exclaimed.

Trent chuckled, "I know, I brought her to you. I need to talk to you for a minute. Let your sisters take Luna for a second."

Shia stopped smiling once she detected the seriousness in Trent's tone. "What's wrong?" She asked suddenly worried as she allowed Remi to remove Luna out of her grasp.

Trent took her hand and led her into the den. "Have a seat."

Shia sat in the chair closest to her wondering what in the world had Trent so uptight.

Rubbing his hands, down his head and face, he looked at her with misery in his gaze, "I did something that you are going to be very upset about."

Shia narrowed her eyes, not uttering a word waiting for him to continue. Whatever it was, she knew that it couldn't possibly be that bad.

"I saw Phylicia."

Shia's blood immediately began to boil, but she was trying to give Trent the benefit of the doubt and listen.

"That's how we got Luna back. You were right. She had her the entire time."

Shia shook her head, not understanding how Trent could still be this stupid when it came to that woman. "We have Luna back. I don't care how you did it. My daughter is home. Whatever it is, I will forgive you."

"I have to go live with Phylicia." Trent sighed.

"WHAT! Are you crazy? You're not going to live with her. You better think again. I'm not having it." Shia jumped out of her chair. "Why the hell did you come in here with that nonsense thinking it was going to fly with me?" She eyeballed Trent incredulously.

"I don't have a choice. Either I go along with her program or she continues to prey on my family. At least this way, you all can live in peace and I'll know you're safe." Trent dropped his head, "I have to keep my family safe, baby. I have to."

Shia knew he was going through an internal struggle, but that didn't make things any easier on her end. She was beside herself and not happy at all.

"Why can't we just report her, and be done with this? You know how to get in contact with her now. Let's end it."

Trent shook his head, "For what purpose? So she can break out again and track us down again? Our whole life has been an ongoing, déjà vu record that I want to end."

"And you think that by giving her what she wants, meaning *you*, it will somehow calm down her psychotic ways? Nothing can tame her, Trent. She is a lost cause and you keep hoping against hope that it will be different. Why?" Shia stared at him, but she knew, "Because you still love her, huh?" Shaking her head, she gazed at him in disappointment. "I should have known. After all these years, you still carry a flame. How pathetic," she looked at him in disgust. "Do what you have to do. I'm done with this. I'm going to spend time with my baby."

Not knowing what else there was to say, Trent gathered his belongings and left the house headed to the address Phylicia had provided him.

****

She had chosen to follow Trent when he left the hotel, knowing that he had been much too eager for her to get a room for that night. Something told Avionne that he wouldn't be returning and it turned out that she was right. *Apparently, I am just that intelligent after all*, she thought smugly.

Avionne watched the family reunion from a distance. With her binoculars, she was able to see inside the home that Trent shared with his family. She keyed in on his perfect little family. *How pathetic*, she thought. No wonder her mother trailed behind Trent, she craved for what he had between his wife and children.

Avionne could understand that. Not too long ago, she wanted some kind of family tie, but not anymore. Love was for the weak spirited and she was anything but that. Once upon a time, Avionne had honestly wanted to get to know her mother. Since life hadn't afforded her the opportunity to do so, she was over it. At twenty, she was a grown woman and no longer believed in fairy tales or the lies they told.

Watching Trent as he left the house with a bag slung over his arm, she started her car and followed him as he drove toward the highway. Glad that she had a full tank of gas, Avionne made sure to trail Trent at a decent distance so he wouldn't know someone was following him. Avionne turned her music up and jammed out with Gwen Stefani the entire ride.

Trent was in his feelings about a multitude of things at the moment. He knew that Shia was writing him off. They were already having a tough time with one another and this change in events wasn't helping any. He did not intend to stay with Phylicia; he was just trying to do what was necessary to keep his family safe for the foreseeable future, buying them all time until he could find a suitable solution that would work for everyone.

Five hours later, after being lost in his thoughts, Trent turned into a cul-de-sac, whereas Avionne kept straight, then looped around the neighborhood and came back; just in time to see her mother look towards her car and close the door.

****

There was a nagging feeling buried at the core of her body. The universe wasn't lining up the way it was supposed to and the feeling forced Phylicia to stay on edge.

"I bet when you went to sleep last night you had no idea that I would be coming for you today."

Phylicia held her head up and stared straight into reflective brown eyes, the ones of her daughter.

"I knew you would come," Phylicia told her softly. "You needed to see me for yourself. I've been waiting for you."

Avionne flinched at her words, "You did not know."

Phylicia smiled, "Of course I knew. You only found me because I wanted you to find me. How else would I receive the opportunity to talk to my baby? You're my flesh and blood. I birthed you. Anything you feel, I feel. I know you better than you think I do. Probably better than you know yourself."

That statement angered Avionne. "I am not your baby! You don't know a thing about me!" Avionne snaked her neck to the side. "Only a mother that raised her daughter would know her child and you are no mother of mine." Avionne spat at her.

"That's where you're wrong. I may not have raised you, but I am most definitely your mother. It is my blood that flows through your veins whether you like it or not and don't you forget it!" Phylicia focused narrow eyes on her. "You turned out just like me anyway." Phylicia said saddened by the reality of what was.

It was taking everything in Avionne not to tear up. This was a poignant moment for her. Her biological mother was standing right in front of her in arms reach and she didn't know if she wanted to hug her or choke her. She couldn't remember her mother's touch and with her so close, she almost let down her guard. Almost.

Phylicia could see the inner struggle in Avionne and she hurt for her. Her daughter was young and still able to feel things. Phylicia commended her for that because around Avionne's age was a pivotal turning point in Phylicia's own life. She went over the deep end and she knew she was wanted by the world and hated by many. The little bit of good left in her didn't want Avionne to turn out as she did. Her baby still had a chance.

"I will never be able to forget that as long as I breathe air into my lungs, I will know that I am your daughter; which means, I will never know peace as long as I live on this earth."

Tears welled in Phylicia's eyes. "Avionne, what is it that you want from me?"

"Nothing. There is nothing you can do for me, mother." She spoke sarcastically, "Birthing me was enough. I guess I should thank you for that, huh? Thank you."

Phylicia stared at the beautiful, angry creature in front of her and became remorseful that she was the reason that Avionne was this way. This is what she had been reduced to … looking at her, Phylicia felt a pang of regret. If she hadn't been chasing behind Trent for years she may have gotten an opportunity to see her daughter grow up and excel in life. *She had the brains to do it, but there is too much me in her*, Phylicia thought, as she refused to give her child the benefit of a response.

"Answer me!" Avionne shouted. "I'm dying over here. I want to hug my mother so bad. I love you, but I hate you too. How could you leave me and never come looking for me? Never check on me? Never wonder if I'm okay? I was left alone in the world. I had no one."

The tears Phylicia had been trying to avoid falling could no longer be contained. "I love you too." She told her baby girl, "I love you so much. I did check on you. I have visited you on your birthday every year since the year I escaped that hospital. Every single year. I have always been in your corner looking out for you. I didn't miss not one birthday. Not one," Phylicia reiterated.

"I saw you graduate high school, early I might add. Very proud mama sitting over here. I saw you graduate college with honors." Phylicia smiled through her tears. "I didn't miss anything. I remember the long pastel, yellow fitted gown you wore to prom with a flower in your hair. My little senorita I called you. You were gorgeous that night."

Avionne gasped in disbelief, "You were there?" She whispered.

"I told you I never missed a moment. If nothing else, I did see my baby grow up. I may have watched from a distance, but I was there."

"That doesn't matter now." Avionne was upset with herself for showing any vulnerability around this woman. "You're the reason my life was as hard as it was."

"How hard was your life really, Avionne? Let's talk about it." Phylicia told her, "Whatever is on your chest just let it out so maybe you can deal with this and move on."

"So who are you, Iyanla now? You think that you can fix my life? Well, you can't! My life is broken and it is your fault. You did this to me."

"Avionne, you're an adult. If something is wrong with your life, fix it. You can't blame me forever."

"This is so comical coming from Phylicia Lynn Taylor. The same woman who spent her whole adult life chasing after a man that never wanted her in the first place."

Avionne's last statement had Phylicia seeing red. "You don't know what you're talking about so I think it's best for you to be quiet now, or did you not get the memo of what happened to your sister?" Phylicia smiled smugly at her.

Avionne laughed, "So you're threatening me now? How typical of you." Shaking her head in disgust, Avionne pulled the gun from behind her back. "You don't know what it takes to be a mother. And I've had enough of you."

Avionne stared Phylicia square in the eye and an unflinching Phylicia stared back at her. She'd known that it would come to this. Avionne had too much rage in her. Phylicia could stop her if she wanted to, but this was one fight she wanted and deserved to lose.

"Good-bye Avi," Phylicia whispered as a single tear slid down her cheek. "I love you. This is the way things should be."

"Good-bye, mother." Avi said, unmoved by her mother's tear.

BANG!

INTRO

Phylicia glared at Avionne as the bullet whizzed past her head at high speeds, grazing her ear, causing drops of blood to drip down her neck.

"You could at least have the decency to know how to shoot in one shot if you're going to be all big and bad, and pull a trigger." Phylicia spat in disgust as she stared into her daughter's emotional brown eyes. An identical replica of herself. *My baby girl. I wish I could have loved you the way you deserved to be loved, but I couldn't,* she thought, as she gazed into the pain-filled soul of her child and saw the internal struggle she was waging with herself. *I just want this to be over. Kill me already; put me out of my misery.*

Phylicia shook her head in disappointment. "You're no daughter of mine shooting like that." Ferociously closing the distance between she and the person that sat in her midst, Avionne knelt in front of Phylicia, so that she could gaze into the woman that gave her life eyes.

"I don't consider myself your daughter, so there is no need to worry about that. My mother died many years ago, but you are a thorn in my side. An itch I have to scratch if you will."

Staring into the heart-shaped face that resembled hers with keen accuracy. "Don't take my missed shot as lack of skill, rather as a sign of remorse as I mourn the lady before me that I will never get to know. A weak moment of consciousness struck me, but don't you worry *mother,"* Avionne closed her eyes and

36

kissed her mother on the cheek. "It's over now. In this world there is no place for the two of us to exist."

It was to Avionne's surprise when moisture formed in her eyes, reflecting on Phylicia's face, mother and daughter eyes, holding, feeling, breath stopped, two tortured souls suspended in time. This was the closest that Avionne had ever felt to Phylicia. Maybe it was the face that Phylicia had given her life and Avionne was going to take hers. There was satisfaction in knowing that her cause of pain and destruction would be no more.

"I could have loved you, you know," Avionne began. "But you didn't want my love, you never did. I have to release both of us from this unhealthy bond."

Phylicia glared at her. "I don't have an unhealthy bond to you," she pointed out. "You came and found me. Placed yourself in my life. I left you to yours; the right thing to do was to leave me to mine.

"Well you shouldn't have." Avionne told her as she stood to her feet. "That was your mistake and I'm over you now." Pulling the .22 caliber up she pulled the trigger and watched undauntedly as the bullet passed between Phylicia's eyes. "Guess I didn't miss that time," she said, as she watched as the body of the lady before her slumped in the chair and blood oozed from the wound in her head. *My due diligence is done. The world is a much better place without her.* Avionne smirked. Looking over at Trent standing in the corner, she waved at him as he scurried out of the house.

"What are you doing here?" Shia eyed Trent as if he had lost his mind, when he walked through the front door.

"You are the same man that told me not too many hours ago that you were going to live a life with Phylicia, were you not?"

"I managed to get away." Trent told her. Choosing to not bring up Phylicia's murder. "I realized there was no way that I could eve leave my family. No way. I love you entirely too much."

Shia gazed up at him warily. All the fight gone out of her body. She had chosen this man and this life, but lately she wasn't sure if he was enough anymore. He choosing Phylicia over her had hurt her to her core. Especially since she had laid it all on the table and went all in with him, only to conclude that he wouldn't do it for her. She would always love him, but was it enough?

"Fine. I'm going to watch TV." Trent quickly pulled her into his arms.

"Please don't act like this. I feel you shutting down on me. I did what I felt was best." He leaned down to kiss her and she allowed it. Even though Shia was upset, her body still reacted to his touch.

"I'm good," she said breaking the kiss. "TV, I'm going to watch it. You can join if you'd like," she called over her shoulder as she retreated to the den.

"That's okay. I have some paperwork that I want to go through."

"Have you seen the news?"

"No. I've been working hard, trying to get the finances in order." Trent replied to Shia without glancing up from the mountain of paperwork on his desk.

"I think you should take a break," Shia told him as she leaned down to plant a soft kiss on his forehead. "And see what information the news is dishing out." She stood straight and winked at him, "trust me, it'll be worth the break."

Looking up, Trent took in Shia's smirk and she winked at him and left the office. Marveling at how, after all this time and all these years, his wife still had the ability to turn him on with a single glance. "Is that right?" he asked, as he pushed in the bank statements and checkbook ledger away on the mahogany wood desk. Trent stood to follow his wife's path to the den

Sitting next to Shia on their plush cinnamon brown sofa, Trent noticed that she had WFMY News 2 turned onto their 65-inch curve Samsung Smart TV.

"Breaking news alert Americas most wanted fugitive Phylicia Taylor have been found murdered in her home this evening. Investigators are currently at the scene more details to follow on the morning news."

Shia eyed Trent's reaction or lack thereof. "Did you know anything about this?"

Trent took his gaze off the TV screen to focus on Shia's inquisitive face. "I may know a thing or two about it."

"What does that mean? How would you know about it? Were you involved or not?"

"Of course I wasn't involved, what kind of man do you think I am?"

"Are you under the impression that I'm mad at you?" Shia asked Trent. "Because I'm not. I just want to know what happened."

"Nothing really happened. She and her daughter went at it and her daughter won. End of discussion."

"And she let you walk away that easily?" Shia stated, ignoring his end of discussion statement. "Even though you're a witness?" Worry laced itself through Shia's voice. From what she had seen of Phylicia, she knew that she was ruthless. Who knows what her seed was capable of?

"Free and clear," Trent nodded.

"That worries me. Things don't usually go that smoothly for us. Especially our family," she emphasized.

Trent pulled Shia into his arms. "Trust Me Baby everything will be ok now. Phylicia is dead. Now our lives can truly begin."

He Loves Me,
He Loves You Not 4

Avionne's Return

The mind is an interesting thing isn't it ...

One moment it can have you seeing and

believing something that's not there ...

The next moment it will have you questioning if

what you see is real ...

The heart works that way to ...

Feeling what it wants to feel ... loving whom it

wants to love ...

Does the mind control the heart ...

Or does the heart control the mind ...

And there lies the true question ...

Isolation becomes me. It is I and I am it. Together we form one entity. One thought. I may not have all of the answers, but I have many. You may think you are more intelligent than I am and I can prove that you are a liar. I can go on and on, but what would that prove? That I am a greater fool than you are? I'll leave you to wonder why I do the things I do and if my mother scarred me for life. The psychologists say she did you know? They think I am a traumatized little girl confined in an adult's body. I'm intelligent enough to know that the information supplied to them supports their theory, but they have yet to interview me and study me to see what really is going on. They are using second-hand information to promote their thesis, while I am here in the flesh and they can study me.

Love me or hate me, you think about me. My mother and I have that sort of impact on the world. We are two peas from the same pod. Even without growing up with her, I ended up acting just like her, maybe more so out of control. Who really knows? What I do know is that you care about me, don't you? You're anxious to see what I am going to do next. Well, I won't keep you. Welcome to Avionne's world. A place for show and tell ... enter at your own risk ...

CHAPTER | 1

I remember the day that I died. The memory replays like an old VHS tape that constantly rewinds itself and the remote is hidden by my little sister Khloe in the deep crevices of her jungle of a playroom. I miss her. Khloe never received the opportunity to grow up. I did that to her. My one contribution to her life. I made sure that she didn't have to grow up with a delusional whore of a mother. I saved her. She'll never know what I did for her, but I take solace in knowing she is free. Free from Phylicia.

Phylicia is a piece of work and by no stretch of the imagination do I mistake the term 'work' as a beautifully depicted oil on canvas painting. Though Phylicia is beautiful and I would be considered a "hater" in today's society if I said anything but. I respect her looks, as a spitting image of her I appreciate the good fortune of having aesthetically pleasing genes. However, as a mother, she is a far cry from stellar. She more reminds me of Faye Dunaway's portrayal of Joan Crawford in *Mommy Dearest*. Sure on the outside she seemed perfect, but inside, oh inside our home was another story. One of retirement and disparity. Never Khloe, just me.

Khloe was crowned with the highest title she could earn, princess, because she belonged to Trent. Trent was everything my mother cared about and as an extension of him; Khloe reaped the benefits. Not I though, never has a human being been more disappointed and angry than my mother on the day she found out that I was not Trent's daughter. I believe if she could have known before birth, she would have aborted me. But I get the last laugh. I am the last one standing if you will, the one able to survive it all.

She took credit for my work and people believed her. How could they do that? In what world are you able to poison a child and not be around to do it? I killed Khloe. I would do it again if given the opportunity. Yes, that is my confession. I could care less if you're upset. Khloe needed saving from this world. I did that. Thank me. I saved her. There was rat poison in her system, of course there was. Phylicia didn't lie about that; she only lied about putting it there. I may have been young, but I knew about many things early in life. I loved playing tea with Khloe. She enjoyed it.

"Avi, it tastes funny."

"It's supposed to taste that way, Princess Khloe. Drink up otherwise I won't play with you anymore."

"No Avi, play with me." Khloe lifted the plastic teacup to her lips and drank, "See, it's all gone. You'll keep playing with me?

"Good job, Princess Khloe. Of course I'll keep playing with you. You're my baby sister after all. I love you."

That day at her dad's though, she was sleeping so peacefully and something came over me. I always

51

wanted to remember her that way, sound asleep. So I took a pillow and gently placed it over her face and sat on it. She gasped for air and that scared me. I removed the pillow from her face and she began coughing. I quickly placed the pillow back over her face to get her to be quiet.

Memories. I said all that to say I miss her. I do believe I did what was best for her, but maybe growing up with a sister that loved me more endlessly could have saved me from becoming the woman that I had become. Or maybe it wouldn't have mattered. I guess we'll never know. All I know to be fact is that Khloe is in a better place than this one and part of me envies that about her. I really do miss her. Khloe, I think about you often and I hope that you think about me as well. Save some space for me up there. One day I hope that I will be able to reunite and be the sisters that the world never afforded us the opportunity to be. My angel, please continue to look over me. I love you forever and always.

CHAPTER | 2

"**H**ey Harris, how is that new case coming along?"

Harris didn't budge as he continued reading the mountain of paperwork that was piled high atop his chestnut, six-foot desk. The guys at the office loved to pick on him since he was new to the division, but he refused to let them get to him.

Graduating at the top of his class, he knew he was the best. That was the reason the captain had sought him out and offered him a lucrative incentive to leave the high-crime area of Memphis and make his way to Maryland.

Though by the looks of the notes that he was reading, he would be traveling to Greensboro, North Carolina soon to do some interviewing. He was one of the individuals that had a fascination with the whole, Phylicia Taylor-phenomenon. It amazed him that this woman had single handedly managed to escape an asylum and then disappear into thin air. One thing he did know was that she had a weakness and his name was Trent.

"Smith, you hear me?"

Harris stopped reading the notes in front of him and have his undivided attention when his captain's vice penetrated his consciousness.

"I'm researching trying to make sense of it all. This is a lot to take in."

"Well here's something new to add to the case, we just heard from Greensboro Police that Phylicia Taylor was finds murdered in her home."

Harris felt a sadness wash over him as he placed the papers that he had absorbed in all day on his desk. Leaning back in his chair he stared at his captain in disbelief. *I'll never get to see her face to face now.*

How does someone on the run managed to only go a few states over, buy a house, and live there without anyone noticing?

"Beats me," was the classless reply that filled his ears.

Staring into his captain's red face, Harris felt as if he were looking at a young Bruce Willis.

"I see why I am needed here. The way, this case has been botched since day one is what gives the media outlets just cause to laugh and make a mockery of us. We have no choice but to take it at this point."

The captain placed his hands on Harris shoulders, "We're counting on you to step in and do what you can. Phylicia has one surviving daughter. You won't find out that much about her from her files because when Ms. Taylor was sent over to the Looney bin, her daughter was put into foster care and then later adopted."

Harris reached for another file on his desk, "I thought her daughter died."

"One did. Suspiciously may I add. But there was an older one that no one tends to mention."

"Avionne," Harris spoke her name as he read Phylicia's medical files and came across a copy of her elder daughter's birth certificate. "Has anyone ever interviewed this girl?"

"Not that I know of," the captain replied. "Instead of being buried under this paperwork, how about you find her and see what she knows or if she knows anything."

"If she's out there, I'll find her. Thanks captain."

"No problem. Give me an update by the end of the day."

"Will do," Harris replied to the captain's retreating back as he turned his attention to the computer screen.

Harris entered Avionne's name into their search system and was able to see that she was adopted at a young age, but that was all. Her files were sealed.

If I was in Avionne's shoes, I do believe that I would have some resentment toward my mother, Harris thought to himself. *Especially once I found out that my mother escaped her lock down at the asylum and hadn't spent one moment of her time looking for me, but had somehow managed to always know where Trent was located every waking minute of his life.*

I need to find her. Time to give Ms. Avionne a visit to see what she's been up to since she dropped out of law school.

CHAPTER | 3

Driving down the deserted one-way street, Harris wondered why anyone would choose to live out amongst the elements like this. Not that he wasn't a fan of nature and singing with the birds, but this reminded him of pure swampland. The stench from the area alone would make the average person say, "No thank you."

Avionne opened the door in anguish, trying to understand why a detective was standing at her door.

"How may I help you?"

"Hello ma'am. Is your name Avionne?"

"Depends on whose asking," Dionne replied leaning onto the doorframe, clad in black spandex shorts and a white tank top without a bra holding up her voluptuous Double-D cup size.

Harris had to admit that this was one attractive woman with her heart-shaped face and sun-kissed skin. There was no denying that she was Phylicia's daughter. Stevie Wonder himself would be able to see the resemblance.

Harris pulled his badge out of his pants pocket, "Detective Harris Smith."

Avionne crossed her arms over her chest, wondering why and how a detective had come to be at her front door.

"May I come in?" Harris asked after Avionne had stood in her doorframe staring at him for the past five minutes in silence.

Avionne had spent the few minutes of silence sizing the detective up. With his Clark Kent good looks and southern charm, he was definitely easy on the eyes. What she couldn't add up though was why he was at her front door and how he managed to find her. She prided herself on living off the grid. She had gone through great lengths to be afforded the luxury of privacy. Two plus two just wasn't adding up to four.

"No." You can tell me what you want from right here," annoyance apparent in her tone.

Harris stared into her defiant brown eyes with sadness. This poor young girl with so much anger and resentment inside of her because of growing up without her mother. He'd been in the force for many years and had seen firsthand what damage that did to someone's psyche.

"Ok. Sure. I have been investigating the care of Phylicia Lynn Taylor, your mother."

Avionne opened her mouth.

"Don't bother denying it." She closed her mouth. "It's obvious I did my research before I came all this way."

Avionne could care less where he came from. All she knew was that he had shown up uninvited.

"I won't deny that she is my birth mother, but my mother, the woman that raised me, Krista died when I graduated from undergrad."

"And yet, ironically your birth mother is also deceased."

Avionne continued to eye him indifferently.

"I'm sorry detective," Avionne kept her perch on the doorframe. "Is there a question you have to ask me? If not, I must be going."

Go and do what? Harris thought. *You live in the sticks with no electricity. What can you possibly be doing?*

"I wanted to ask questions about you, your childhood, and about your biological mother. If that's all right. Would it be okay if we did this inside?" Harris asked her again hoping that she would give in as he began to perspire heavily under his suit in this humid North Carolina weather.

"No, it's not okay. Stop trying to get in my house goodness. I've said all I am going to say. Have a good day Detective."

Harris watched as the old metal rusted door closed with a snap in his face. Then turned to walk down the five wooden steps and began walking around the shack of a house.

Avionne followed Harris' movements from inside her home. She'd built her home with necessary holes to serve as windows. She kept a close watch as he circled the house a couple of times and finally got his fill and left. Avionne knew a problem when she encountered one and Detective Harris Smith was definitely going to be a problem and she was going to have to nip it in the bud.

CHAPTER |4

Avionne loved the thrill of the chase. There was nothing like it in the world. Watching, as the delightfully blissful couple exited the shopping mall and walked to their car holding hands and gazing into each other's eyes. Avionne knew they only had a matter of time left and she was almost gleeful that they had no idea they were only a few moments left in their lives. Truly hope that they are enjoying this time they have together.

Dodging in between cars as she slowly crept up on them. She wrote down the license plate of the Burgundy Dodge Caravan; that screamed soccer mom all over it. *I live for this,* she thought, as she watched him pull away

Walking back to her car, she wondered what it could feel like to have someone love her. She'd never given it serious thought.

"Fancy seeing you here."

The voice startled Avionne out of her own head. She groaned inwardly and looked up.

"What are you doing here?" She eyed him warily. "Why do you insist on bothering me? What do you want?" she asked exasperated. She knew that she had recognized the voice.

"I'm just trying to see what a lady such as yourself is doing creeping around the parking lot." His voice one of suspicion, wondering why she was crouched in-between the cars.

"I'm minding my business if you *must* know." She glared at him. "I wasn't aware that I was of such interest to you. Last time I checked, stalking is a crime. You should not be following me," she pointed out.

Harris gazed into the direction that Avionne was coming from, trying to figure out what she had been doing out here on the ground. Maybe she really had come to the mall, but if that was the case why didn't she have any shopping bags?

"You are aware that it's a free country right? I was not stalking you; it's just mere coincidence that we are in the same place at the same time." He looked pointedly at her empty hands; did you decide you didn't want anything at the mall today?"

Avionne sighed loudly as she used the keypad to unlock her black Nissan Maxima, shaking her head at her bad luck. She was going to have to find a way to make Harris back off of her, so that she could do what she needed to do tonight. He was definitely too close for her comfort. She was feeling smothered.

"No, I didn't see anything that I wanted." Avionne sighed in resignation. "What can I help you with Harris?"

"I was wondering if we could maybe go to dinner."

Alarm bells began to sound in Avionne's head. Why would the good detective want to go to dinner with her?

Avionne began looking around suspiciously, hoping this wasn't some type if a set-up.

"Are you looking for something?"

"I'm just trying to figure out if Ashton Kutcher is going to jump out from behind one of these cars, because I'm obviously being punked. Where is the camera crew? Y'all got me." She clapped her hands and stomped her feet.

Harris feigned innocence. "That was a genuine offer. I'm a little hurt by your response." And to his surprise, he really was. He was interested in knowing more about Avionne and seeing if she was anything like her mother.

Avionne didn't know what to think. "I have plans for the night actually, but maybe we can go tomorrow night if that works for you."

Harris face lightened, "Tomorrow is good for me." He was ecstatic. She had finally agreed to something.

"Great, so now will you stop stalking me? Avionne faked laughed.

"Trust me, if I wanted to stalk you, I wouldn't let you know about it." Harris tipped his hat at her and walked away. His gut was telling him that Avionne was up to something tonight and he was going to get to the bottom of it. Moving swiftly in the parking lot, he jumped into his borrowed Greensboro police cruiser, so that he could observe Avionne, and see what she was really up to. Eyebrows furring up, he saw her get into her car and pull off. His antenna was up high. She'd seemed suspicious when he had approached her. Turning the key in the ignition,

Harris waited for the cruiser to purr to life before following the path he'd driven only the day before.

Tonight was the night. Not one to let anyone ruin her plans, she put the encounter with Harris out of her mind. Avionne was dressed in black attire, long hair pulled into a ponytail, ski mask, and her black duffle bag of goodies. She was anxious to get the evening started.

Throwing the bag into the backseat of her car, Avionne got situated in the driver's seat, put on one of her favorite musical pieces by Bach, Toccata, and Fugue in D-minor. She loved to listen to this classical number before each of her joyous, anxiety relief filled nights.

Swaying her head from side to side and closing her eyes, she allowed the music to wash over her, consume her. Reach into her blood and flow through her veins.

Yes, this is what life is all about. Waiting for the classic to go into repeat, she started the car and backed out of her dirt driveway.

Watching through binoculars from a tree that he had climbed adjacent to Avionne's house, he watched as she put a bag in the backseat and then sat in her car with her eyes closed for a few minutes. *What are you up to little lady?* He was itching to know.

Oblivious to the fact that she was being watched, Avionne fed off the energy of the music radiating through her car. She was ironically calm; her mother's death being a few months prior, she'd made it a priority to lay low. Especially with Detective Smith always lurking around and snooping in her space, but tonight was a perfect night

to do what needed to be done. A great night for a kill.

CHAPTER | 5

"Mama."

"Hi my little munchkin." Shia smiled as she leaned down to scoop Luna into her arms. Luna promptly lay her head on her mother's shoulder and Shia kissed her forehead. She treasured moments like these more than anything in the world.

"There are my two favorite ladies in the universe." Trent smiled as he entered the master bedroom of the house to find Luna and Shia hugged up together on their plush pillow top king bed.

"How long are you going to continue to hold her? She looks as if she's been asleep for a while."

"I know, but she's getting so big. In a little while, she won't let me hold her like this anymore. So I'm enjoying it for now."

Trent smiled, "I know, but I'm going to put her to bed now, okay? We need some adult time." His voice deepened.

"Oh do we now?" Shia asked seductively. "Well under those circumstances I can let her go. How can a girl refuse such an offer?" She gazed down at a peacefully sleeping Luna, kissing her on the forehead again. "Here take her before I change my mind and neglect you of my wifely duties."

Trent laughed and Shia passed Luna to him. "I'll be right back beautiful," he smiled knowingly at his wife.

"And I'll be right here when you return." She returned his smile with sparkling eyes.

After ten minutes passed, Shia left the bedroom to locate her husband. Making her way down the long hallway to the last bedroom that was Luna's, she was surprised to see the door shut. *That's strange.*

"Baby what you doing in here?" She asked as she opened the door and began to walk in, but then stopped short.

"If you scream, I will break her neck. Do you understand?"

Shia nodded at the woman holding her sleeping baby in her arms as she chose to remain silent. Her eyes darted to the large bloody heap on the floor in front of her. *Oh no Trent. Not you baby.* Her mind was screaming.

"Close the door," Avionne commanded.

Shia did as told with no hesitation. Luna's life depended on it.

"I want to start by saying that this isn't personal. I'm so sorry my mother chose your husband to stick her grimy claws into. I'm apologizing on her behalf." Avionne laid Luna down in her toddler bed. As she raised the gun with a silencer attached. "I'm not one to hurt children anymore. I can't handle it. Too bad I can't say the same for you however."

Shia made a diving attempt towards Trent to see if he was breathing, but the bullet connecting with her brain stopped her cold.

And yet once again, my work here is done. Maybe I should go into retirement. Avionne almost laughed out loud at herself as she backed out of the window from whilst she came. *Nah, the works needs me.*

CHAPTER | 6

At the restaurant, Harris thought about how he'd been unable to climb out of the tree without being noticed the night before, which had forced him to lose Avionne once she drove off into the night. But all night, he couldn't sleep wondering where she had gone and what she was up to.

"This is nice. Thank you. I'm so glad I took you up on your invite," Avionne smiled up at him.

Harris returned her smile. He hated to admit it to himself, but he was extremely attracted to her. There was an aloofness about her that beckoned him. She intrigued him. He felt as though he needed to know everything about her. He knew his interest bordered on obsession.

He had been obsessed with her mother Phylicia and that had somehow passed itself on to her. He felt if he could learn more about Avionne then maybe he could truly understand Phylicia and get some insight into his infatuation with her. The two of them were an enigmatic puzzle to him and he knew he wouldn't be satisfied until he could figure out all the pieces. He knew as a detective that he was crossing the line by playing with fire. But he also knew that he needed to do whatever possible to make a break in his case. So that meant that he had to sacrifice himself for the cause and he was willing to do just that.

"I'm glad you did too. I've been looking forward to this."

Avionne had given the whole Detective Smith thing some thought and figured that it would be much better to have an inside man with law enforcement because she was bound to have things that needed fixing a time or two to help keep her out of jail. She thought of him as an investment to her freedom. And one thing she knew about investing is that they typically paid off in the end, so they were always worth it.

"I'm not going to lie to you, I haven't, but now that I'm here, I'm happy to be here," was her honest reply.

Harris could only chuckle to himself. He had to give it to her she didn't mince words. He always knew exactly what she was feeling and he admired that about her. He knew plenty of grown men who had trouble saying exactly what they felt, so the fact that a woman could do it impressed him. She was a refreshing person to be around.

"Why are you so anxious to get me out here on a date?"

"Who said anything about it being a date? I just asked you out to dinner to get to know you a little better and maybe to have you more comfortable instead of coming in to the station."

"Oh, so this is more like an interrogation? Be it a nice one, it is still an interrogation."

"I wouldn't necessarily say that. I just want you to feel as if you are in a safe zone. Hopefully one day you can think of me more as a friend."

Almost snorting out loud, Avionne caught herself. As if someone like her needed friends. What she needed was an ally with the law and he was going to give her that. Whether he wanted to or not.

"Of course we can be friends," she told Harris in a singsong voice, as she forced a smile. She was more than equipped to play this game as well. She wanted to see how far he would go to get close to her to learn more about her mother and possibly her.

Observing her forced smile, Harris knew that she didn't mean it. He knew a user when he saw one, but on some level, she had to have feelings. Right? That's the woman he needed to get to know. Somehow, he was going to have to break past her tough exterior and get to the soft interior he hoped that she possessed. And one thing he loved was a challenge.

Avionne had never been to Ruth's Chris Steakhouse. She took in the ambiance and wondered how Greensboro, North Carolina had this. She'd seen many of them up north in the city, but she was shocked to see it in the south.

"I want to thank you for joining me this evening."

"Can we PLEASE bypass the pleasantries? We both know you brought me here to find out more information about my mother. Besides the fact that she's dead, I have nothing else to contribute to your conversation."

"How did she die?" Harris pressed her. They made a breakthrough. She'd been the first to bring up her mother this time and he was going to run with that small sign of encouragement.

"You tell me. You're the detective. I saw it on the news and only know the details that everyone else knows," she lied. There was no way that she could tell him she blew Phylicia's head off for being an unfit mother. There was also no way to tell him that she regretted it. She wanted and missed her mom. She wished she hadn't been so impulsive and they could have talked some things through.

"Is that right?"

Eyeing him intently, Avionne wonder what it was that he thought that he knew.

"Yes, that is right," she stated mildly agitated.

"Thank you," Avionne and Harris spoke in unison when the waiter came and filled the glasses with water.

"My pleasure. Are you ready to order?" the waiter asked.

"Yes," Harris immediately responded.

"No," Avionne told the waiter.

"We'll have two orders of your ribeye with asparagus and broil tomatoes," Harris told the waiter ignoring Avionne's response. "Please bring us both a Caesar salad to begin thank you."

"How dare you order for me? You have no right." Avionne hissed at Harris once the waiter had left their table.

"Because we're not wasting time since you're acting like a spoiled brat."

Eyes flashing in anger as Avionne stood, "You sir may eat alone. No one tells me what to do, ever. Have a goodnight." She stomped off and Harrison let her go.

"Oh, but they will. But they will," he spoke softly in her wake.

CHAPTER | 7

My heart is so broken. What are we going to do without Shia? This is crazy. Who would do something like this to them? I don't know what to do. Leigh's emotions were all over the place.

She was at a loss for words. The news was unbearable to her. How does one continue life without the other half of their heart? She was a twin;

what do you do when your twin is no more? She was half of a whole and she would never be complete again. Her heart couldn't take the pain.

Walking over to Remi, Leigh pulled her into a hug for a lack of knowing what else she could do to ease her pain. She didn't have an answer for this senseless act of violence. There was no way to make sense of it all. No way at all.

"Help me understand Leigh. Who is going to tell those beautiful babies what happened to their wonderful parents. And Luna is so young, what about her? First, she gets kidnapped and now her mom and dad are gone. Remi shook her head in disbelief. "This is craziness. Will our family ever know what peace is? Or will we always be cursed? Almost as if we were cursed from the beginning."

Leigh held on tighter to her baby sister, allowing Remi's tears to sooth her. She had yet to cry. She wasn't sure if she was in shock or what was going on. But a pain this intense, she wasn't sure if tears were enough to cover it.

"Remi, don't try to make sense of it, because we will never be able to understand. We'll never know why people do the things they do or why our family was chosen for this life of turmoil." Leigh rubbed Remi's hair and closed her eyes, "All we can do is continue living. That's it. Hope for better tomorrows."

"If this is what tomorrow brings, I'd rather let go of this life we living today."

Leigh grabbed Remi's shoulders and shook her hard, "Don't ever let me hear you talk like that! Do you hear me! Never say those words again!" Leigh was borderline hysterical; losing her mind at the words that Remi had just spoken.

Remi's tear soaked eyes stared into the nervousness and worry etched on Leigh's face and she felt horrible for the words that she'd just spoken.

"I'm sorry Lei Lei, but this is all too much,"

"It is too much," Leigh agreed. "But I can't lose another sister. I just can't."

"I know you can't and I'm so sorry that I said something like that to you. I take it all back. You and our nieces and nephews are definitely worth living for and I will never forget that."

"Thank you for appreciating that we are all the family that have left. We have to make a pact that we will stick together no matter what. I need you in my life, forever. You, the kids, all of it – we have to get through this. You know that Shia and Trent would want us to."

Remi lowered her head ashamed of herself. The hurt consuming her was forcing her to talk crazy. She never wanted to end her life she just wanted a way to bring Shia back.

"I know. I'm sorry. I was talking crazy. It wasn't my intention to scare you."

"I know it wasn't and I don't hold it against you."

"Good. Because ain't nobody got time for that," Remi sassed Leigh giving a hint of a smile.

Leigh's mouth sprung into a toothy grin at Remi's statement, "See that's the sister I know and love."

"Nothing can hold us down. I love you." Remi told Leigh as she grabbed her hand.

****

"When can we go?"

"Shhh! Don't be rude." Leigh was irritated by Remi's comment. She was barely hanging on by a thread and it seemed as if after the initial shock, Remi had gotten over Shia and Trent's death rather quickly. See, Leigh thought that's what mashes us different. There's a special bond between twins. Even siblings couldn't understand.

Staring at poster size photos of Shia with white roses under each one, it was taking everything within Leigh to hold out together. The memorial service for Shia and Trent was sad at best. No one was there but she, Remi, and Shia's children, because they were still in the witness protection program and had no friends present.

This is way too much, Leigh thought to herself as she allowed the tears to flow down her face. Walking slowly over to a photo that the two of them has taken recently, Leigh stood in front of it gazing at her beloved twin's face.

"Shia I will always love you," she whispered. "Every time I laugh, I'll know you're up there laughing with me. Every time I cry, I know you're sharing my pain. My whole world, my life was wrapped up in you. My beautiful angel ... taken from us too soon. You never deserved this." Leigh's sobs were loud, echoing across the garden. "Why couldn't it have been me? You're the one with the family. It should have been me."

Leigh stiffened when she felt little arms grab her leg and squeeze. "It's ok Auntie Lei Lei. Don't cry."

Bending down to embrace Luna, she smiled. "Thank

you auntie's baby. That's exactly what I needed."

CHAPTER | 8

The breeze was a perfect complement to the warm day, as the mourning family gathered to pay their last respects at Center City Park. Avionne watched them at the memorial service as she stood in the back of the park with her dark shades on, trying to not seem too conspicuous. Personally, she didn't have a vendetta against Shia's sisters. She didn't have one against Shia. Shia's only crime had been loving Trent. It had been necessary to murder Trent. Phylicia had dedicated her life to loving Trent and Trent only. There had never been room in her heart for anyone else. Phylicia was unable to be a good mother because of him and as Avionne saw it, that meant that he needed to join Phylicia in the afterlife. She had considered sparing his life, but she needed the pain to end and she had thought killing him and the woman he loved more than anything would curb that pain but it did nothing but intensify it.

Why can't I be happy? Because you were never taught true happiness. You wanted your mommy and she wasn't there, her subconscious whispered to her. *Why would I want that whore? You don't know what you're talking about. Really? So what are you looking for? A way to end that emptiness and despair? You killed the only person who could give*

you that. Are you satisfied with yourself?

Avionne wished her subconscious knew when to let bygones be bygones and shut up.

Staring at Shia's sister across the way, she could feel the sorrow in one of them more than the other could. Aww she's snotting all over the place, how unattractive of her, Avionne thought. Someone should teach her how to be a lady. I know her sister died and all, but is that seriously a reason to lose your cool and be in public looking a fool? Avionne shook her head in disgust. These women today really needed to learn a thing or two about decorum.

Following the women as they separated from the young people who were ushered into a car and off the premises, the women chose to huddle up and talk.

Avionne wondered what kind of a pow-wow they were having.

Moving slowly towards the women, she marveled at fate. *I came to enjoy festivities, but since they've opened themselves up as bait, I'd be a fool not to take them up on their offer.*

Creeping up on women, she took out her weapon of choice and aimed it at the two of them. As they continued to talk, she released the weapon and watched as it soared through the air connecting with the snot nose sister.

Jackpot! One hitter quitter. *Damn that girl has got aim.* She complimented herself.

A shrill scream could be heard as the unharmed sister dropped to the ground doing surveillance of her surroundings as she shouted Leigh's name over and over again.

Keeping to the perimeter of the trees, she moved in for the kill shot of the other sister. A smile mirroring the Joker radiated from Avionne's face. She was having a blast.

CHAPTER | 9

"Leigh, you've got to fight through this," Remi cried in vein. "This is me and you. If you leave me I will have no one. What am I supposed to do without you? I need you. We just lost saw Shia and Trent. I need you to not die on me." Remi felt as if her world was slipping away. Now that Shia was gone, Leigh was all she had left. "You cannot die on me," she said to Leigh. "You just can't." Remi lay her body across Leigh's trying to keep her warm. She knew that she needed to take this time to say goodbye to her sister. With blood oozing out of Leigh's mouth, Remi knew it was over. She didn't care that her clothes were now blood-soaked. She was just trying to make sense of it all. How does she go from being the baby sister to the only sister in a matter of weeks? The twins have been around her whole life and she needed them as you need air to breathe. She didn't know the first thing about being anyone's mother, and while the boys were pretty much independent enough to take care of themselves, Luna was another story altogether. Remi knew that she was now going to have to strap it down, buckle it in, and be an adult. She didn't know if she was up to the challenge. Kissing her sisters cool lips when we allow the tears the fall, but she knew she had to get going before the murderer came back and found her.

"I love you Leigh, with everything in me, and nothing will ever change that. But I have to go. I will never forget you. You and Shia will always mean the world to me."

Getting up swiftly off the ground, Remi took off running. She knew her killer was still out there, stalking and waiting to find her. She had to get as far away from this place as she could. She couldn't believe that this was happening on the same day that they had to bury Trent and Shia. The heart of the family.

Hearing nothing but silence, Remi stopped running. She needed to know what was going on around her. Silence was a bad thing, it meant that the killer was waiting and watching so that they could go for the kill shot at any moment. Moving her head from side to side, she needed somewhere that she could hide. Looming before her was a massive tree, she remembered her mother always saying that she reminded her of a monkey because she was always climbing all over the place. Remi thoroughly hoped that still applied and that she remembered how to climb a tree.

Avionne took surveillance of the ground, looking for her prey. But she didn't worry that she had momentarily lost sight of her. She knew that it was only a matter of time before she surfaced; and one thing Avionne prided herself on was patience.

Remi scurried up the tree, proud of herself for being able to still do it after all of this time. Her proud moment quickly turned into panic as she stared into the eyes of the person who had killed Leigh and was chasing her.

Avionne smiled at her good fortune as her prey climbed up onto the tree branch next to her. *Well look at that ... there must be a God after all,* she silently rejoiced. Her excitement was short lived however, as her prey leapt out of the tree and fell to the ground.

Remi hit the ground hard. She knew her shoulder had to have broken, though it was pure adrenaline getting her through. A sense of urgency and survival. She had to make it out of here alive. She owed it to her nieces and nephews.

Jumping to her feet with cat like reflexes, she thanked God that she was an avid runner. Using all the strength that she could muster up, she ran as hard and fast as she could toward the highway.

Avionne was in heaven. *She loved when her prey ran. It makes this cat and mouse game that much more exciting,* she thought as she raced in sync parallel to Remi with a smile on her face.

"I'm gonna get you," she sang as she leapt through the air, pretending as if she was the key ballerina in a solo performance.

Remi ignored her as she continued the race of her life. She had survived worse situations, she'd be damned if this psycho bitch got the best of her.

After what seemed like an eternity with the psycho chick, dancing and leaping beside her, Remi could finally see headlights. Waving her hands frantically she prayed for someone to stop. But everyone continued rolling along right past her.

Avionne stopped dancing so that she could retrieve the bow and arrow that she carried on her back. Sad that the chase had come to an end. She placed her arrow in the bow and upon release watched as it sliced through the hair, missing her prey by a hair. "No daughter of mine would have missed," Avionne could hear Phylicia's voice saying to her. *Get out of my head. I didn't miss the second time when it came to you mother.* Avionne smirked as that statement of truth silenced the voices.

Remi felt the arrow whiz past her and gazed in horror as it crashed into a car. *I have got to get away from this girl.* She waved down the next car, which turned out to be a police car, and thanked the lucky stars that God was finally smiling upon her.

Harris stopped his car when he saw a young woman waving anxiously in the street.

"Miss, what's wrong?"

Taking in the woman's disheveled appearance; he knew she had seen better days. She was none the worse for wear.

"Someone is trying to kill me. Please ... Please help me." She screamed out as she gasped for air.

Harris immediately reached for his gun as he unlocked the door to let her into his borrowed cruiser.

"You'll be safe ma'am." He recognized the woman, but didn't want to alarm her as to how he knew who she was. He looked in the direction that she came from and didn't see anything. "What direction was the perpetrator coming from?"

"She was right beside me. She killed my sister. Leigh's body is out there somewhere." Remi pointed in the direction of the trees. "Please get me out of here. I'm scared," she replied as she looked around, hoping her killer didn't sneak up on the car.

"Ok, ok. I'll make sure you're kept safe. Nothing will happen to you now. I'm going to call some back up, okay?" Harris told her. "I promise not to leave you."

Avionne watched in disbelief as Harris' car pulled up and a sprinting Remi managed to get saved. She snapped her fingers as she faded back into the woods. *I'll get you next time and trust me, next time I won't miss.*

CHAPTER | 10

S he knew that she was skating on thin ice, but she took the risk of inviting him on a dinner date at her house anyway. Nothing beats a failure but a try. Nothing.

"I really appreciate you joining me this evening. Thank you," she told him seductively.

Harris took in Avionne's short and tight white dress that hugged her curves and smoky eyed makeup. The way she was being nice to him made him wonder what had changed in their relationship so to speak.

He knew she was up to something. He always felt that way around her, as if she was constantly trying to get over all the time.

"My pleasure," Harris said as the dinner that she prepared lay before them on the dinner table.

"I hope that you brought your appetite, because I'm ready to feed you."

"Is that so?" Harrison looked at her suspiciously. "What's with the new change of heart?" he asked her.

"I just want to do something nice for you." She smiled over at him. "Is that so bad? I mean is that a crime?"

"Of course not. It just seems out of the ordinary for you," Harris told her she, as she prepared their plates for dinner. "Last time I saw you, you stomped out on me at dinner."

"Oh come now. Let that go. You knew that one day we would eventually end up here."

"And where is here exactly?" Harris inquired.

"You at my place, like this. You know you wanted me since you first laid eyes on me on my doorstep. I saw the way that you admired my body. And when my nipples got hard the way you wanted to suck on them," her voice was low and seductive. "I know you want me Harris, you don't have to fake it. It does put you in an awkward situation however. A detective falling for the woman that he suspects of murder." She turned sympathetic eyes on him. "What is a man to do?"

Harris was shocked. "I never suspected that you were a murderer. I just wanted to know more about you and your mom. Touch base on some things."

"Oh come now, Harris. You're a bad liar. To be such a recognized and honored detective that you are. I expected more from you."

Harris wisely said nothing as he continued to regard Avionne, waiting to hear what it was that she was going to say next.

"Of course I did my research on you Harris. I needed to know who were and where you came from. Everyone that enters my world is subject to a thorough background investigation. You must understand that and come to know that it's just how I am."

Harris remained silent, as he made sure that the safety was off of his gun just in case he was prompted to use it.

"And guess what I found out?" Avionne continued as she took the knife in her hand and sliced into the lamb chop that she had prepared for their dinner. "I found out that you used to be married, but you're not now. Your wife died in childbirth. That must have hurt," she told him, genuinely sad for him. Avionne gazed at him expectantly.

"Yes as a matter of fact it did," Harris said on cue. *It hurt like hell. Still hurts. I miss my wife.* He wondered where she was going with this conversation.

"I am truly sorry for your loss. I lost a sister once; it is a tough thing to get over. I'm not even sure if a lifetime is long enough. I'm still affected by it."

Harris continued to look at Avionne wondering what she was going to do or say next. The girl was an enigma.

"Why do you keep watching me like that?" Avionne asked him. I saw that you took the safety off your gun. Harris I'm not trying to do anything to you. I just want to feed you some good dinner, maybe give you some good head, and call it a night."

Harris' body immediately reacted to her statement. He knew that Avionne was dangerous. But the thrill of her was exciting. He needed to know all about her.

"You know, you shouldn't lead a man on like that," he said laughing, relaxing a little, but keeping the safety off his weapon just in case he needed it. "Don't be surprised if I take you up on your offer."

"Nothing surprises me ever." Avionne told him in all seriousness. "I'm always ready for the unexpected. No matter what is going on in my life, I am always on guard. And in no way, shape, or form am I leading you on. I meant exactly what I said and I always back up my word.

Harris stood up swiftly from the table. "Then why are we wasting time?" In one motion, he had moved around the table and swept Avionne up into his arms.

Using one arm to push the dishes and food to the side, he lay Avionne on the middle of the table.

"This is what you want?" he asked her, as he pushed her red lace panties to the side and inserted two fingers into her moistness.

"Yes," Avionne moaned as her body arched on the table. She had been missing this in her life. She couldn't remember the last time she'd had a man to please her.

The evening was beginning to look up, she thought as she and Harris' bodies moved in sync to the dancing candlelight; dinner was long forgotten.

CHAPTER | 11

"Y'all have got to move faster than that," Remi told her twin nephews, as she clutched tightly to Luna's hand. Remi wasn't taking any chances; she wanted to get the children as far away from Greensboro, North Carolina as she could. She was done believing in and counting on the federal government's witness protection program.

Where had that gotten any of them? Her whole family was gone, all because Trent had the misfortune of meeting Phylicia years prior. It wasn't bad enough that they spent years looking over their shoulder because of her, now her psychotic daughter was an issue. The cycle had to end. The children deserved a normal life. Especially Luna. She was new to the world and in her few years on earth, she had been in the witness protection program, kidnapped, and now she was on the run. Remi shook her head at the fate of the world. The stars were never in alignment with her family that she could see. Her mother having an affair cursed their family forever. The universe was mad at them and Remi didn't have the slightest clue on how to fix it.

"Auntie, I'm tired," Luna screeched, as she held onto the pink bunny Remi had picked up for her at the newsstand in Raleigh Durham airport.

"I know you are baby. We are almost there."

"I'm getting sick of this," one of the twins stated.

Remi closed her eyes praying for patience. She never asked to be in this role. She never contemplated having children. After the life she had, she wasn't sure she could trust anyone enough to procreate with them and risk being tied down to them forever.

"I'm sick of it to," she told him. "I am so sorry that you all have to go through something like this, but I'm doing the best I can," Remi told him

Both put on their *Beats by Dre* headphones and tuned her out.

She above anyone understood the kid's frustration. They were angry and needed someone to take it out on, and she was the last one person standing, so she knew she was going to have to take the brunt of it for a while. They hadn't even gotten the opportunity to attend a funeral for Leigh. Her body was sitting in the morgue, waiting to be claimed. *I'm sorry Lei Lei we just can't risk it. I love you always.*

They boarded the plane with nothing but carry-on bags because she had told them to grab what they could. They were off to a new beginning and she was grateful for the opportunity to have her surviving family disappear so that they may finally know some peace.

CHAPTER | 12

Walking around the park that she had previously killed one of the sisters in, Avionne truly felt at peace. There was always something free about nature that she enjoyed. She could stay in the wonderland all day. That's what nature was to her, a wonderland of possibilities, and a great burying ground.

"Oh my gosh! Avi is that you?"

Shocked that someone would recognize her enough to call her by her nickname, Avionne glanced up in surprise, and a smile paraded across her face.

"Kamila? What in the world are you doing here?" she asked in disbelief.

"Well I heard that you may be in the area so I came out here to check for myself."

Avionne pulled her into a hug. "I'm so happy that you're here. This is amazing. I'm sorry to have left the way I did when ma died, but I couldn't stay there. It was too much for me then and too much for me now."

"I know," Kamilah told her. "I didn't stay long after you left. She was our glue, you know? Once she was gone and you were gone, I had no idea what to do with myself. So I made it my business to find you. And trust me; you are a tough lady to track down."

"Obviously not tough enough. How did you find me?" Avionne needed to know, because if it was this easy for Kamilah to find her maybe she needed to give some thought to potentially relocating soon.

"Come on Avionne, seriously? I know a lot about you. Especially your obsession with your biological mother. So I started by trying to find out her whereabouts. Then I read about her murder and I knew you had to be close. No one wanted your mother dead more than you. It was like you sent me a smoke signal and here I am."

"Are you implying that I had something to do with that?" Avionne asked innocently. "I loved my mother Kamilah, biological or otherwise. I know nothing of what you speak of."

124

"I'm not implying at all. Implying is for people who aren't sure. I am very sure and stating facts. I believe you had everything to do with it." Kamilah gazed at her through long lashes. "I told you, I know you better than you know yourself. We grew up in the same household remember? The keeper of each other's secrets."

Avionne began to regard Kamilah in a whole new light. Growing up, she had always seemed so naive, but naivety was not the word to describe Kamilah at all. Calculating was a much better word. Avionne made a mental note to not lose sight of that.

"I'm not passing judgment Avionne," aware that studying her, not saying a word. Which was not a good thing when it came to Avionne. A talking Avionne was better than a silent one any day. "If my mother weren't already a victim of the streets, I would have killed her myself. I get it. This is a no judgment zone."

Avionne studied Kamilah for a moment longer before deciding that she could probably trust her. Kamilah hadn't gone to the police or shared her whereabouts with anyone and Avionne was going to make sure it stayed that way.

"That's good to know. So you've found me, what is your plan while you're here?" she asked Kamilah.

"I want to stay with you," Kamilah announced. Hoping that Avionne allowed it. She had nowhere else to go. The money she had stolen she had to leave behind in order to flee. She had taken just enough to get her here to Avionne.

Avionne cut her eyes at Kamilah. "Stay with me? Why?" The last thing she needed was a houseguest.

"Because," Kamilah looked down at the ground. "You're the only family I have and I need someone. It's lonely out here. I have nowhere else to go. I'm homeless."

"I'm not sure if that's a good idea," Avionne told her as her attention shifted to the children playing on the monkey bars and their mother standing there encouraging them. Suddenly, she had an idea, a change of heart if you will.

"Ok, you can stay. Under one condition," Avionne's wide grin encouraging her.

"What's that?" Kamilah asked suspiciously, wondering why Avionne was cheesing at her and shifted gears so quickly.

"See that mother over there?" Avionne pointed to the petite Asian woman in the distance playing with her three children. Kamilah nodded. "Good. If you kill her you can stay."

Kamilah followed the stretch of Avionne's finger. "You want me to what?" she was in disbelief.

"Kill her," Avionne smirked. "I need to think of you as an asset versus a liability. So that means you have to do that one thing and then you can say. It's up to you. Like an initiation into a gang or something." Avionne raised her eyebrow. If Kamilah wanted to stay with her, she was going to have to show her what she was made of. "If you don't, there are no hard feelings. You'll go your way and I'll go mine."

"I don't know about this Avi. I just really need somewhere to stay. I'm not down with killing people."

"I'm not changing my mind. You're the one that needs somewhere to stay, and if you want to stay with me, those are the conditions. So if I were you I would get to getting. I have to get home to cook my dinner soon."

"Fine," Kamilah obliged. "Right now?" she inquired. "No time to plan this out first?"

"Now."

"Now?" Kamilah's eyes widened, but she's playing with her kids Avi. "How do you expect me to do that? And do you really want it to be this woman? We know what it's like to grow up without mothers and to be put into the system. Do you really want them to go through that?"

"Look, not my kids, not my problem," Avionne was unsympathetic. Who cared if these kids lost their mother? The state would get them a new one.

And if it didn't work out that way, tough. Mother's weren't all that cracked up to be anyway. Avionne couldn't understand the hype. "If you want to stay, you'll figure it out. Once you're done, we'll meet in the parking lot and I'll show you my house. Otherwise, it was nice to see you again. You have fifteen minutes to get it done and then I'm leaving."

Kamilah knew this was a test. Avionne was giving her a chance to kill or be killed. *Little does she know that I'm up for the challenge.*

"I'll be waiting for you." Avionne winked at her, and then strolled to the parking lot.

CHAPTER | 13

Kamilah watched the family for a while, fully aware that Avionne was in the distance watching her. *What am I going to do?* What she hadn't told Avionne is that the reason she had sought her out was because she was wanted in five states. New York, New Jersey, Pennsylvania, Virginia, and Connecticut. To say that she was a fugitive was putting it mildly. See had banked on Avionne not watching TV too much. Bank robbing was her thing, but a murderer she was not. However, she also knew that Avionne was ruthless. And she meant what she said. Looking at the young woman playing with her family, Kamilah felt bad for her. She looked so happy. Her only crime being bringing her children to the park that day to play. The kids looked so free and full of life. Blinking back tears, Kamilah knew that she had to do what must be done. She knew this would be a day that the unsuspecting lady's children would never forget.

Reaching into her purse Kamilah pulled out a handful of taffy. She had loved taffy growing up and figured the children would to.

"You sure do have some amazing kids," Kamilah told the woman as she approached them playing on the monkey bars.

"Thank you miss," the woman smiled appreciatively. "They are my world. Do you have children?"

"Not yet," Kamilah smiled, showing off her dimple. "I can't wait to be a mom though," she lied. Having children was the furthest thing from her mind at the moment.

"It's the best thing in the world," the woman smiled back. "I'm Melinda by the way."

"Sybil," Kamilah responded.

"Nice to meet you Sybil."

"Likewise," Kamilah told her, as she sat Indian-style on the ground.

Glancing at the children to make sure they were okay, Melinda joined Kamilah on the grass.

Kamilah was banking on that. She loved the south and the south's unreserved ability to talk to and befriend anyone.

"You from around here?" Melinda asked her. As her short, black bob swayed in the wind.

"No, I'm from up north. Down here visiting friends. I'm thinking about moving here. Trying to get a feel for the area."

"Well welcome," Melinda exclaimed. "You'll love it here. It's so peaceful and serene."

"I'm loving it already. You're the first person that I've met. Thank you for taking the time out of your day to talk to me."

"Oh absolutely. I love meeting new people. Especially nice ones and I can tell that you're a very nice girl."

Kamilah wanted to roll her eyes at that. This woman had no discernment whatsoever. If she really knew why Kamilah was there, she would run for the hills.

"I brought some taffy. I'm not sure if it's the goods kind though." She opened her hand to show Melinda.

"Oh that's a saltwater taffy. That is the best kind," Melinda exclaimed.

"Really? That's good to know. Would you like one?"

"Oh absolutely. My children love this stuff."

"Do they? I have more in my car. Do you want to come get some that you can take home for them?"

Melinda looked at her kids one more time, "Ok sure, while they're still playing and not thinking about me, I'll run to the parking lot with you really quick."

Kamilah couldn't believe her good fortune. "Great. We'll be right back," she told Melinda standing to her feet.

"I'm right behind you Sybil."

As they moved toward the parking lot, Kamilah steered them toward the trees. "I always cut through here, it's faster."

"Oh me too. I do it all the time," Melinda laughed.

As soon as they were out of sight from her children, Kamilah lurched at Melinda, passing one hand around her head and the other over her mouth. Twisting her head in a swift motion to the left, she heard the snap indicating that Melinda's neck was broken. Removing her hand she lowered the body to the ground and continued walking toward the parking lot as if nothing was out of the ordinary.

Standing in front of her clapping and paying homage was Avionne. "Bravo Kami, bravo. You have a place to sleep tonight. Let's go."

CHAPTER | 14

"Hi," Kamilah said, her eyes taking in the handsome man standing at Avionne's door, with his curly hair and caramel complexion.

Harris was taken back when the attractive brunette answered Avionne's door.

"Hello."

Kamilah smiled at his obvious discomfort. "May I help you?"

"Yes. I apologize for being rude. Is Avionne around?"

"Yes, my sister is around. Come in," Kamilah waved him into the house. Stepping back so that Harris could enter. *Sister.* He thought her only sister had died.

Harris fought the urge to glance at Kamilah, clad in only a loose fitting tank top and boxer briefs.

"She's in the kitchen cooking dinner. I think she was a chef in another life. She cooks every day of the week," Kamilah laughed

Harris offered no reply as he entered the kitchen, and just as Kamilah had stated, Avionne was at the stove, cooking something up. He stopped to appreciate her scantily clad body in a white tank top and blue biker shorts before speaking.

"Hi beautiful," Harris approached Avionne from behind to give her a hug.

"You're not getting attached are you?" Avionne asked as she backed away from the hug. She didn't allow herself to forget for a second that Harris worked for the opposite end of the law than she did.

Harris stepped back. He knew his place, but he found it hard to decipher right and wrong when he was around her.

"Who was that who answered your door?"

"Oh, just my adopted sister Kamilah," Avionne told him. "Why do you ask?"

Harris shrugged, "Just curious I guess."

"Oh, don't be curious." She spoke softly, "I don't like it." And she didn't. Kamilah was an attention whore and Avionne knew that her seeing Harris was going to create problems between the two of them.

"Why? You're the one that doesn't want me to get attached or anything right?" Harris pointed out."

"Never mind. Do what you want," Avionne feigned annoyance.

"Come here," Harris said, as he walked up to her kissing the back of her neck.

"Come up to the room with me," she told him, as she lifted her tank top over her head, affording him a look at her perky breasts.

Following her out of the kitchen while she was topless was the highlight of Harris' day. Watching the way her back curved to present the perfect arch was a definite turn on. He wanted all of her and he wanted her now. Lifting her off her feet, he spun her around, ran her full length over top of his as he sat down in the dingy hallway, and kissed her lips. He'd been dreaming of this since the one previous time she had allowed him to touch her like this before. No one knew how to ration out loving better than Avionne.

"Kiss me," he demanded. "His body was crying out for hers. Avionne happily obliged him. It was unclear to her why she couldn't just give in to this man. *What am I saying? He wants to find dirt on you to have you locked up in jail.* Never forget that. *How can I forget? You are always hovering over me, reminding me.* She and her subconscious were waging a war and Harris was none the wiser as she kissed him with enough ardor to have him forget that Kamilah was even in the house.

142

"You want to do this here?" Avionne asked him breaking their kiss. "Like right here on the stairs."

"Right here on the stairs," Harris told her.

Avionne shrugged. She didn't mind Kamilah walking up on them or hearing them. The girl probably needed to learn a thing or two.

"Take these shorts off." Avionne did as she was told. She enjoyed Harris like this. This was the one time that she let him be in charge and she loved his authoritativeness.

Harris' eyes absorbed her body in one fluid gaze. Her waist was so small that he could wrap both his hand around it and have them touch.

"You have an amazing body," he told her. He hadn't really got to see too much of it the first time they had got it in on her kitchen table. Eyeing her

Brazilian wax, he knew he was going to have to have a taste.

"Thank you. Running seven miles a day will do that for you," Avionne smiled. She knew that her body was fabulous. She wasn't lazy by any means and her body reflected that. "Well you've got me out of my clothes, what would you like to do with me?" She asked.

Harris leaned back, "I want you to come stand on this step where may head is and squat on my face."

"Mmmm your wish is my command boo." Once again, Avionne did as told. As soon as he squatted on Harris' face, he put his tongue to work and Avionne had to hold on to his hair to keep her balance. "Oh yes. Yess. Yessss," she screamed.

"What the hell!" Kamilah's voice broke through Avionne's haze. "Y'all are disgusting."

"No one said that you had to watch," Avionne told her in between breaths as she began panting loudly enjoying putting on a show for Kamilah and experiencing the beginnings of her orgasm.

Kamilah stood there, watching the two of them not care that she was still in the house let alone the same room.

"Y'all some freaks," she told them, as she walked away after watching Harris make Avionne cum. The whole erotic play made her want Harris even more. At the very least, she knew he was good at making his mouth work.

"That was crazy," Avionne said as she stood on wobbly legs trying to regain her composure.

"I agree," Harris told her. He had never engaged in any form of sexual activity with someone watching.

145

"I'm not in the mood to reciprocate today," Avionne told him. "But I am down to sit on it if you like."

"I do like," Harris told her as he unbuckled his pants, slightly taken aback that she wouldn't return the oral favor. He would settle for a good ole ride however.

Once Harris had taken his pants off and sat back on the step, Avionne straddled him and began riding him like a horse at a rodeo. *This is fun,* she thought. *I may have to keep him around for this purpose alone.*

Later that evening, Avionne could see the attraction sparking between the two of them and it was affecting her mood, making her more and more irritated. She had half a mind to chop both their heads off, but decided against it.

146

"You make the best dinner, though I didn't get to partake in it last time. What I did partake of was very adequate however." Harris smiled into Avionne's direction as he took another bite of his steak and mashed potatoes.

Avionne smiled as she cut her eyes at Kamilah, who had yet to remove her gaze from Harris. *Did you hear that bitch?*

Kamilah was knee deep in the Harris sauce. Whatever he was, she wanted to smoke it all day long. His high was intoxicating. So engrossed was she, that she was not mindful of Avionne's seething rage that she was barely containing.

Harris knew a threatening sign when he saw one. Avionne felt as if Kamilah was a threat to her and Harris was doing what he could to make sure she knew there was no need to be threatened. Avionne needed to know that she had his undivided attention.

Once he'd gotten over his initial shock of seeing another woman answer Avionne's door, he had recognized her.

She was Kamilah Wright, a known bank robber wanted in three states that he knew of, maybe more. He didn't know her whole background, but he was going to make sure to make it his business to find out.

Out here in the sticks was a great place to run, but he'd bet a million bucks she wasn't banking on a detective from up north knowing about her or being down here in these sticks as well. He decided to keep it on the low who he was for now.

"Tell me more about yourself," Kamilah interrupted Harris' thoughts.

"What is it that you would like to know?" Aware that Avionne body language was adjusting to a fighting stance.

"She doesn't need to know anything," Avionne shot a pointed look at Kamilah

"Excuse me." Kamilah said as she promptly left the table.

"You're excused?" Avionne told her with her attitude apparent.

"You don't have to act like this," Harris informed her. "She's no threat to you."

"Oh I know she's not, but she needs to understand that flirting with you won't be tolerated," Avionne informed him.

"You staking claim now?"

"Hardly. There is no way someone like me could stake claim over someone like you. Likewise with

Kamilah. We have too many demons to try and live a normal life."

"You want to tell me about it?" Harris interjected hoping she would open up to him and give him something concrete to use against her.

"No." *I'm not stupid fool.* "Nothing at all." She smirked. *He is trying to play me. I will never forget for one second who you are boo. Your sole propose is to bring me know down. And my sole purpose is to use you for my own benefit.*

For him to have researched her so much, it amazed Avionne that he didn't yet understand that she was the queen of the cat and mouse game. Manipulation was her strong suit. *Patience Harris, patience. You'll get what you want so badly. I'll see to it.*

150

CHAPTER | 15

Remi and the children were living it up in Malibu, a beach in Southern California, finally getting an opportunity to enjoy life and not be looking over their shoulder every time they turned around.

"You seem to be enjoying yourself."

Remi looked up when she heard the deep masculine voice.

"I am immensely," she smiled up at the handsome face wondering where he had appeared.

"I love to see pretty women enjoying themselves," the handsome stranger continued.

Remi was horrified to find herself blushing. She couldn't remember the last time a man had flirted with her. She was horrified at the prospect. She wasn't sure if she knew how to flirt back. *How pathetic am I?*

The fact that he found her pretty, with her black and red spiked hair, tattooed art all over her body, and dramatic face piercings, she had just added the studs to her cheeks, she thought he was either amazing or lying through his teeth to try and impress her.

"May I join you?" he asked after a moment.

"Sure. But I must warn you I'm here with my nieces and nephews," she pointed in the distance at a trio making a sandcastle.

"That's okay, I love children. But I'm here to see you." He sat down and studied her expressions.

His last statement raised Remi's suspicions. Who was he?

"Why?" She asked him.

"Because I've been sent here to help you," he told her.

Help me how? she wondered. "What is it that you think I need help with?"

"Your life. Let me introduce myself. I'm a friend of the guy, Harris, who saved you that night you were running for your life. My name is Nathan, but you can call me Nate."

Remi sighed in disbelief. "How did you find me? I thought I did a good job of getting the kids away from Greensboro without making any noise or causing attention to ourselves."

He gave her a slanted look, "I commend your efforts, but you left a paper trail. You bought your plane tickets with a credit card and you were seen on the camera. For future reference, always pay with cash and then no one will find you."

"Duly noted. So what is it that you want to help me do?"

"I want to help you survive, but I also want you to help me get the person who is targeting your family."

"I know who the person is. It's no mystery. It's a generational curse that began with her mom, and now with her, and if she has kids, her kids will

154

probably prey on my nieces and nephews. It's like an ongoing non-stop horror film; they will not end. This family needs peace, haven't we lost enough already?"

Nate could understand her pain. And he was damned if, for the first time in his career, he really wanted to help someone outside of the usual protocol.

"I think you shouldn't have to run anymore. What if I promise to protect you? Would you believe me? I will take you and your family in. You'll be part of the witness protection program until we get this situation handle, but at least you'll be with me. I won't leave you by yourself. I promise."

Mouth dropping open in shock, Remi couldn't believe what she was hearing. Are you serious? Like for real serious? Like this isn't a joke or game you're not playing with my emotions. You're serious, like this is good money; I could take this to the track and bet on it?"

Nathan chucked to himself. He loved her personality. When his captain had sent him out here to follow up on the case, he had no idea it would be this fun or that he would now have long-term houseguests. He knew his captain wasn't going to take too kindly to that part.

"You can definitely take this to the bank and cash it in. Every check I write is good money. And my word is solid gold."

"How do I know that I can trust you? Our family doesn't trust easily. We've been through a lot of bad things that have happened to us. And I know you're a man that's taken an oath to uphold the law and everything, but there are corrupt people working in uniform as well." She couldn't help that she was jaded. Everyone was suspicious or guilty to her until proven otherwise.

"I promise you that I am trustworthy. You can have access to my files if you like. Come talk to my captain and friend's if you need references."

Smiling a genuine smile for the first time in a long time, Remi relaxed as she watched Luna and the twins continue building a sandcastle.

"Thank you," she told Nathan, as tears slid down her cheeks. "Thank you for making me feel safe. I appreciate you for seeming like someone that I can trust."

"My pleasure ma'am, my pleasure," Nathan told her.

CHAPTER | 16

"What is the deal with you and Harris anyway?" Kamilah asked Avionne.

"There is no deal, but he's off limits to you and I need you to backup." Avionne let her know without glancing up from the rope she was tying together.

"No need to get your panties all uptight about it. I was just asking a question," Kamilah snapped.

"I'm not understanding why this is even a discussion," Avionne told her. "If you want to date somebody go date somebody. I don't care what you do, just lay low, don't get caught, but Harris is not the one that you can date end of discussion. Do you understand?"

Kamilah sliced her eyes at Avionne, but didn't utter a word. *Crazy bitch.*

Her silence is what made Avionne finally look up. "I'm going to need a response to that question," she stated, looking Kamilah straight in the eye daring her to go against what she had been told.

"I hear you loud and clear my dear," was Kamilah's smug response.

Avionne and Kamilah held each other's gaze. "Kami, try me if you must. But I don't recommend it to be in your best interest to do so," was Avionne's sweet reply.

Kamilah broke their gaze first. "There you go, always trying to get violent. You've marked you're territory you sick bloodhound. I won't tempt Harris. He's off limits. I got it. I'll go find my own man," she says smartly, before turning and exiting the room.

"Good girl," Avionne watched her go and knew that she was going to be a problem. She loved her adopted sister, the same way she had loved Khloe, her biological one, and that still didn't save Khloe from her fate. Kamilah better tread lightly for Avionne excelled at sending people to meet their maker.

"What is it that you do for fun?" Kamilah asked Harris intentionally antagonizing Avionne; as the three of them sat down to enjoy their fish tacos that

Avionne had made for dinner. Kamilah seemed to have bumped her pretty little head on the back of a chair.

The way that she kept smiling up in Harris' face, Avionne knew that it was time to pay the piper.

Standing slowly, with the rope concealed in her hand, she began a death march to Kamilah's chair.

The two of them were having such a great time, engaging each other in conversation that they weren't paying her any mind.

In one fluid motion, Avionne raised her hands and had the rope around Kamilah's neck in no time.

Harris stood to his feet attempting to draw his gun, but realized he'd left it in his car.

Avionne's gaze caught his and he stopped moving.

"I'd hate to have to kill you Harris and you know I'm good for it. Sit down and enjoy your dinner." She spoke calm and deliberate. Her promise lingering in the air.

She pulled the rope with all her might as Kamilah's survival instincts kicked in and she tried unsuccessfully to get the rope untangled from her neck. Avionne's determined fingers pulled until she saw Kamilah's face go white and her body limp.

Harris looked at the dead body slumped in front of them. Avionne followed his glaze.

"I don't know what happened to me," she said as she released the rope. "She just makes me so angry," Avionne told him indifferently. "She was wearing out her welcome anyway. I was tired of her."

He was in disbelief that Avionne would kill right in front of him. "I'm so sorry that you did that right

162

in front of me. I'm going to have to take you in. You do realize that do you not?"

"Harris, honey think about this first. Do you really think you want to go this route?"

Shaking his head 'no', Harris remembering that he had another gun strapped to his ankle, now that he could think more clearly pulled it out and leveraged it on her. "Turn around. I'm going to have to cuff you."

"I like it when you talk nasty to me," she smirked. Avionne had known that it would finally come to this.

She turned slowly and presented Harris with her back as she placed her hands behind her.

"It's one thing for me to think you're guilty, is a whole other story for you to prove it too me," he said solemnly.

"Are you certain that you want too cuff the mother of your child like this?" she whispered. "How do you think our child would feel about that, when they find out eventually that you are the one that put their mother in jail?"

Her words stopped Harris cold. *What child? Please God no. She can't be saying what I think she's saying. She can't be pregnant. She can't be. God work with me on this one. I know I do a lot of things that I shouldn't do. But this punishment doesn't warrant the crime.*

"Our little love muffin. The life that you and I created when you were panting hot wanting Kamilah, but too much of a coward to tell me as such. Why do you think I jumped on you that night and made you forget all about her?"

For the first time in his life, Harris wanted to do bodily harm to a woman. He was enraged by the chain of events taking place. Avionne's conniving little mind had thought everything through. He knew she had intentionally gotten pregnant so that he wouldn't be able to take her to jail. But he was as much at fault as she was and he knew that. *Why didn't I use a condom? Cause you're an idiot.* He grew more and more irritated as she continued smiling that smug smile at him. He wanted to wring her neck.

"You psychotic bitch," he growled for lack of better words and he had always prided himself on being a gentleman. She had reduced him to this.

"It's okay, I'm not offended. I've been called worse, except in this instance, I'm the mother of your child," she smiled a loving smile at Harris. "Now, how are you going to explain that to your captain? Huh?" "The way I see it, you should just settle down and eat your food. I'm thinking about a very large nursery. What do you think?"

Harris was stuck in his own head. He'd forgotten to ask about his captain. Unable to remember the last time he'd checked in. His captain was going to throw the book at him once he found out how deep Harris was in the situation. He had violated protocol. Under no circumstances was he to engage in a relationship of any kind with a potential murderer. "I'm so screwed," he stated.

Avionne smirked as she left Kamilah's face in her food and pulled Harris's head to her chest to try and get him to relax.

"Oh come now, boo. It will be all right. It's only a baby."

Harris pulled out of her embrace." It's not just a baby. It's a life that I do not want to have with you."

I want to kill you, he thought. Which was another first. He'd come down here to get a better understanding of Phylicia and her daughter Avionne, and now he was leaving as a pawn in her sick and twisted game of life. His child's information would now be a part of their police file, his as well.

He shook his head in disbelief, "I can't believe I was so stupid." He stood abruptly, forcing his chair to fall back and crash to the floor. "I'm going home."

"Home is where the heart is and I have your heart inside of me. You can't leave me." Avionne replied, still smug about the situation.

"I don't plan to. You're coming with me," he told her. "Pack up what you can. We're leaving now."

"Ooooh, I love it when you man up, Daddy."

Avionne smiled. "There's nothing I need more than this. Let's go."

"Here hold this for me." Pulling an item out of her waistband, she handed the positive pregnancy test to him as a souvenir.

CHAPTER | 17

I'*m going to have to kill him,* she thought which was sad, because besides being a detective he was a really nice guy. But he was too focused on the avenging Phylicia's murder, as well as Trent and Shia, and there was no way she could allow him to send her to jail. In another life, she and Detective Harris would have been perfect for each other, but in this life this one right here, there was no way they could possibly be. *I wish I had been born to someone else that way I would have been afforded the opportunity of a normal life. But unfortunately for him I wasn't and now every single one of his days as number, I'm going to have to let him go.*

Avionne was beside herself as she went about her shopping habits of going into the Home Depot to get her materials ready. She didn't know what day she was going to do it yet, but she knew him never to believe the day was coming.

Harris wasn't a fool. He knew that he was making Avionne more and more uncomfortable. He was banking on their relationship to help her cope through this and to get him the information that he needed to ultimately put her away.

He'd be lying if he said that wasn't a part of him that truly did love her and he knew a part of her truly love him as well, but they just weren't meant to be. There was no way that he is sworn to uphold the law. How could he be with someone who was a sociopath and didn't have a problem killing who ever stood in her way? And knowing Avionne like he thought he did, and after all the countless hours of research that he had done on her, he knew by the way she operated, that it was more than likely going to come down to a fight of the other half of the will sooner than later and he knew he had to stay on his guard and be ready at all times.

*****

She couldn't stand to see people happy. It was as if them being happy somehow took away moments from her life and she wasn't going to have anyone removing moments from her life her mother had removed enough of them as it was. If she couldn't find the will to be happy, no one deserve the right to be happy, as far as she was concerned. Following the couple that just left the bookstore, Avionne had located her next target. A little snack to make her feel better.

CHAPTER 18

Relaxing in his own home, Harris knew that he had made a mockery of being a detective. When his superiors learned of the situation, they were going to lock him away in the penitentiary and throw away the key after they made sure that he was buried in the deepest part of it first.

He was consumed with guilt. How could he not have been smarter than this? He should have known that Avionne's devious mind always had a plan. He'd spent countless hours studying her and her mother. He knew better and yet he had fallen prey to her web of lies anyway. All for what? To be sitting here, agonizing over how his life ended in shambles.

Staring into his glass of Hennessey straight up, he was thinking and plotting on his own.

"Hey baby, would you like something to eat?" Avionne asked sweetly.

Willing his eyes to focus on Avionne in his drunken stupor, he had to admit that even though he hated her, she was radiant pregnant. Being with child suited her, not that she wasn't beautiful to begin with. Clothed in a flowing white maxi dress, hair pulled up into a bun on the top of her head, face devoid of make-up, she seemed almost normal.

"No," his stomach growled in protest, but he didn't care. He would starve before he let Avionne feed him another thing to eat.

"Baby, stop acting like that. I know you're hungry. I can hear your stomach growling from over here," she told him, as she continued whipping mashed potatoes into a pan.

"I don't want your food. You can go to hell," Harris spat at her.

"Fine, have it your way," she told him. "Sit over there and starve for all I care."

Harris went back to the drink in his hands, wondering if he was on the way to becoming an alcoholic. He was pretty sure drinking day and night made him a qualifying candidate.

The steel bowl that Avionne had in her hands clamored to the floor as she yelled out in pain and grabbed the bottom of her stomach.

"Oh my god, oh my god, oh my god. Help me," she screeched, as she slid to the floor balling her body up into the fetal position.

Harris jumped up of the sofa when he saw her lay down on the floor, grabbing her stomach.

"What is it? What's wrong?" he asked her calmly. He was trained to remain cool in situations like these.

"I'm hurting so bad. Help me. Please, oh my god. Help me. Please. Something is wrong. Please Harris. Please," she moaned, consumed in pain.

Kneeling down to the ground Harris did his best to access what was going on, but when he moved her hands, he saw little dots of blood lining the floor.

"We have to get you to a hospital," he said, as he lifted her into his arms.

Anne Arundel Medical Center

"She has to be placed on bedrest," the doctor informed Harris. "Her body is trying to hemorrhage and push the baby out. We're going to keep her here for a few days to observe her in hopes that we can get that to stop. But she's going to have to take it easy."

Harris wanted to laugh hysterically. Avionne didn't know the first thing about taking it easy and he was the one stressed out, not her.

"Thanks doc," Harris said to the doctor as he walked him out into the hall.

"Exactly when were you going to tell me about this?"

Harris' blood ran cold when he heard his captain's voice. Harris had been avoiding him. It was D-day. Turning around, he was ready to accept his fate.

"Smith, what the hell were you thinking?" his captain demanded

"Honestly, I wasn't doing much thinking sir. As proven my whereabouts right now," Harris replied.

"You know I brought you on my team because you came highly recommended from Memphis. The accolades you received stretches states over. So I took a chance on you. I believed in you. And this is what you do? You sleep with someone you're trying to bust for murder? What the hell happened down there in North Carolina?"

Harris felt like a five-year-old getting lectured by his father.

"It never should have happened. I don't know what came over me. I got caught up in something bigger than I could control."

"You're damn right it shouldn't have happened. You know what else shouldn't have happened, you shouldn't have been hiding this girl in your house and not saying anything. You've been back for mouths. I have a revolving door and a damn good ear."

"You're absolutely right captain. I'm an idiot. I haven't been coping well with this situation."

"You're damn right you're an idiot. And more so than that, I'm suspending you without pay pending an investigation into your actions while you were down in the sticks and since you've been back. Turn in your badge and your weapon."

Harris was in shock. "You're suspending me?" He echoed as he placed his badge and weapon into the captin's waiting hands.

"I'm disappointed in you, Smith. You need to do some soul searching and find out which side of the law you want to end up on. Take it easy."

Harris watched his captains retreating back and mentally kicked himself. Avionne was making a mockery of his life in more ways than one.

CHAPTER | 19

"Congratulations! You have a son," the doctor announced. Harris wanted to rejoice. A son.

They were in the operating room where Avionne had an emergency C-section because the baby's heartbeat was dropping.

"Thank you Jesus for keeping him here with us," was all Harris could muster up as his little screaming bundle was placed in his arms. He'd never been so happy to hear a crying baby in all his life.

"How is she doing?" Harris asked the doctor.

"She's going to be alright. Lost a lot of blood, but we're going to take good care of her."

"When can she hold him?"

"When we get her all settled. Won't be too much longer now," the doctor told him.

"Great news," Harris responded.

"Knock, knock, you have visitors," a nurse announced from the doorway.

Avionne looked away from her son smiling. Her smile slipped away once she saw the officers at her door.

"Hello miss. You are being placed under arrest."

Harris smiled, as his police buddies entered. He couldn't allow Avionne to mess with his livelihood. As a measure of good faith, he had told his Captain about the murder of Kamilah Wright and agreed to have Avionne arrested as soon as she had the baby and was clear to leave the hospital.

"You have the right to remain silent. Anything you say can and will be used against you in a court of law. You have the right to an attorney. If you cannot afford an attorney, one will be provided for you. Do you understand the rights I have just read to you? With these rights in mind, do you wish to speak to me?" the officer asked Avionne.

"No, I do not choose to speak with you." Avionne glanced over at Harris, "What is happening? Did you know anything about this?" She snapped at him. "I just had my baby. The doctor won't allow it."

"Why are you asking me about your situation?" he asked her with a grin. "I'm not the one arresting you."

Avionne narrowed her eyes as she took in Harris's grinning face. *So you want to play hardball,* she thought.

"How can I be under arrest? I've done nothing wrong," she politely told the officers, choosing to ignore Harris.

"Do you know someone by the name Kamilah Wright, ma'am?"

That little shit. She frowned up her face. "I have an adopted sister by that name," she told them.

"You killed her. They have the body. It's over Avionne," Harris told her pointblank, sick of playing games with her.

Oh, you're damn right it is. Your life will be over. She glared at Harris. "I have no idea what you're talking about."

"That's fine, you don't have to. These nice boys are going to wait with you until the doctor allows you to leave and then they will take you away anyway." Harris winked at her. "They're hoping that they will be able to jog your memory."

"Ma'am, please stand."

"I've just had surgery," Avionne's anguished reply resonated off the walls. "You can't do this. What about my son?"

"He's my son to. We'll be fine without you."

185

"You will not get away with this." Avionne hissed.

Harris continued smiling as he heard the handcuffs chick around her wrists. Justice was finally being done and he was ecstatic about it. Cradling his son in his arms, he knew that all would be right in the world after all.

CHAPTER | 20

Harris was enjoying the dad life. His son Jaxon was his whole world. Only two months old, and Jaxon was already holding his head up, smiling, and responding to his dad's voice. "I love you little guy."

"Aww, what's going on in here?"

Harris smiled at the sound of Payton's voice. Payton was his girlfriend and she had been the godsend he needed after his momentary lapse of judgment with Avionne. Payton was a nurse at Anne Arundel Medical Center where Jaxon was born. She'd been present the day his buddies had taken Avionne into custody and had felt compassion for Harris. Payton had stepped right in to fill the void of Jaxon being motherless.

"Someone enjoying Papa time?" Payton asked.

"You know it. I can't get enough if this little guy."

"And he obviously can't get enough of you either," she laughed.

"That's a great thing," Harris responded, as Jaxon began yawning in his arms.

"I'm going to put this sleepy punkin down for a nap before I head out on my trip."

"Okay," Harris said handing Jaxon to Payton; loathe letting his son go for even a moment, but understanding that naptime was a valuable part of his day. Babies are so addictive. *Who would have thought that I would actually love this whole parenting thing.*

Retrieving the mail from the kitchen counter, he noticed a letter from Avionne. He had to give her credit that she was one persistent woman. He received a letter every day that the mail ran, six days a week from her. Usually he tossed them into the trash, but his curiosity was getting the best of him. What is it that she possibly had to say every day of the week?

Harris,

I know that we have our differences and you feel as if I'm undeserving of your time, but can you please send me a photo of our son? Please put yourself in my shoes for one second. I haven't seen my baby boy since he was four days old and ripped away from me. Please Harris, just one photo. I'm begging you and I've never begged anyone for anything. I'm his mother. I can survive where I am if I just have something to hold on to. Please allow me the opportunity to see his face. Do you realize that I have no idea how my baby boy looks? None whatsoever. I know someone in there that you have a heart. Maybe a misplaced sense of trust, but a good heart nevertheless.

At least consider it.

xoxoxoxoxo

Avi

Harris lay her letter on the table as he gave her request some thought. In all honesty, what would it hurt to let a mother see a photo of the child that she had birthed? It's not as if she were going to get a chance to hold him, her name wasn't even on the birth certificate, so there really was no way for her to stake claim over Jaxon.

I can oblige her and send one photo, he thought. *Yeah that's what I'll do. What can on photo hurt?*

****

"What you in for?" a heavy southern accent questioned her.

Ignoring the tall freckle-faced, red head, Avionne wasn't in the mood to a conversation with anyone. The police in Maryland had extradited her back to North Carolina to let their police force handle the murder case they had against her for Kamilah. A case that her baby daddy, Harris was going to testify in. *I so disappointed in myself. They caught me slipping. It won't happen again.*

"When someone speaks to you, its impolite to not respond," the red head continued, beginning to irk Avionne's nerves.

"Murder," Avionne's cold hard stare met the surprised one of the red head. *Exactly bitch. Back up off me.* "Any other questions?"

Her inquisitive fellow inmate became moot after that and walked away. *Good. Teach you to be in others people business. I never not one time asked what got anyone else put in here because I don't care.* Hair braided straight back like Queen Latifah's in the movie Set It Off, no make-up, an orange jump suit, white socks, and Nike slides, Avionne felt as if she had never been the worse for wear. Rapidly losing weight due to the fact that she refused to eat any of the food provided to her for fear of food poisoning.

After dinner, Avionne was glad to be back in her cell. She needed to concentrate on a plan to get out of this place and make her way back to Maryland, so that she could see her son. Picking up the photo that Harris had sent her in the mail, her heart melted every time she gazed at her baby boy. She was grateful that Harris had finally deemed it necessary for her to see what her baby looked like. She had begged him enough in all of the letters that she had written him.

She found it amazing how much that her priorities had changed with the birth of her baby. She wanted to be with her son all the time. She would have been able to handle this place if it weren't for that, but with her seed being out in the world without her she needed to be with him. He was a part of her and she craved the sight of him. While in the hospital she'd called him Lucas, but she knew for a fact that Harris had named him Jaxon Harris Smith, but she didn't care. He would always be Lucas to her. The losers in Maryland hadn't even allowed her time to sign her baby's birth certificate. *Bastards.*

Sitting on the bunk, she pulled her sketch of the Sheriff's Prison Farm out from under her mattress. While living in Greensboro, she'd studied and converted to memory the blueprints of each facility in the event that she was ever caught for any of her fun escapades, that she enjoyed partaking in. In her spare time, she had previously tunneled through the entire prison center so that she could have an escape route. Her only question was when she would have an opportunity to pull off this illustrious stunt.

"Avionne, you have a visitor."

Great.

After finishing with her security check, Avionne checked in at the visitor's desk and smiled when she saw her guest waiting for her.

"Get up and give me a hug, Chicca!"

Her visitor laughed as she stood, "Same crazy Avi I see."

"Payton, girl, it has been a long time," she said as they sat down. "How are things out in Maryland?"

"Girl, your baby is the most adorable little sumo wrestler in the world."

"Oh, I bet he is. Even though I don't think little and sumo wrestler belong in the same sentence," Avionne laughed. "I'm so jealous you get to see him every day. Thank you so much for halting your life for me."

"It is never a problem ever. What else are cousins supposed to do if they don't help one another out?

Family over everything, honey. Plus your baby daddy is one fine piece of work. I don't mind sopping him up with good loving every night." Payton laughed.

"Gross, "Avionne frowned her face up. "Please spare me the details. I know what it's like and you need to remember not to get too attached to him. He's a dead man walking."

"I know, I know. I'm just helping to make his last days a little more pleasant."

Avionne burst into laughter. "Payton you are good and crazy, you know that?"

"So I've been told." She leaned in across the table and spoke lowly, "So, what's the plan? When we getting you out of here?"

"Tonight."

"Tonight? Ok cool. Same plan?

"Yup. You know what to do."

"Yes ma'am, no worries. I'll be seeing you tonight then."

"Yes you will boo," Avionne smiled, grateful for Payton's undying loyalty.

She hadn't seen or spoken to Payton in years. Payton was one of her adopted cousins and the two of them had naturally clicked when they were smaller. They lost contact after Payton graduated high school. She was a little older than Avionne and had left for nursing school. Which is the one thing that had come in handy when Avionne was in this latest crunch. She hadn't trusted Harris during her entire pregnancy. She knew that he would ultimately pull some ookie doke move and bless the baby monkey if she hadn't been right. She'd had Payton on stand-by for that purpose. Payton had transferred

197

into Anne Arundel once Avionne had been put on bedrest and the rest is history. *I'm always thinking a head boo.* She knew that Harris continually underestimated her, which is something that she couldn't understand. For him to have such an obsession with her mother, he sure couldn't tell that the apple didn't fall far from the tree. She was constantly able to pull the wool over his eyes at every turn.

"Now please, tell me more about my gorgeous baby! I cannot wait to see him tomorrow."

"Oh, I can go on and on," Payton began gushing.

CHAPTER | 21

S itting in the nursery, rocking Jaxon back and forth, as he read him a Mother Goose tale, Harris looked up when he heard a noise down the stairs. Checking the time on his watch, he saw that it was 3:30 in the morning.

"Hey babe, is that you?" Payton had said that she would be back in the wee hours of the morning.

"Yes boo, I'm coming up now," the familiar voice called out to him and his baby relaxed. Even though he knew that Avionne was locked up, sometimes he was still on edge. It wasn't that he was afraid of her; he had been in the force for over ten years. She was more so just an unsettling spirit to be around.

"Did you miss me?"

The hairs on the back of Harris' neck prickled when he heard that voice. The voice he was dreading, Jaxon's mother. Avionne.

Squeezing his baby tightly to him. Harris glared at Avionne.

"What are you doing here? I know for a fact that they didn't just let you walk out of that jail down there." Harris was pissed off. Avionne was like a roach. No matter how much you stomped on her, she seemed to reappear everywhere.

Avionne shrugged, "I had other plans. They'll be looking for me soon, so I won't stay to bother you. I just came to get my son and we can all go our separate ways."

"You'll want to do what she says. It's two of us and one of you. We will win." Harris gaze switched to Payton.

"What does our situation have to do with you? And what do you me it's "two of us"? You're working with Avionne?"

Payton smiled, "How else do you think she got here? We always put family first."

"Family?" Harris whispered. "Y'all are related?"

"Now for a man who prides himself on research," Avionne began as she started approaching him.

"You sure didn't do your homework." As much as she loved banter, she didn't have time today. She had to get her child and get as far away from this place as she possibly could.

Harris held Jaxon closer, "You won't get away with this."

"Fuck," Avian took out her gun with a silencer attached to it and shot Harris in the head. She grabbed her son before he fell to the floor. "Didn't I tell you I didn't have time? Now look what you made me do." She scolded Harris' dead body. "You done gone off, and got yourself shot." She shook her head. "Men." She looked over at Payton in exasperation, "What is it that they expect us to do with them? We give them chance after chance and they still act a fool."

"I know," Payton said, nodding in agreement. "Here, take this bag. It has everything you need to get away from here and everything your son needs as well."

"You're not coming?" Avionne asked, as she reached for the bag, no time to enjoy the feel of her baby boy in her arms.

"No," Payton shook her head. "You go ahead. I'm going to stay here and deal with this mess. Try to give you more time to get to where you're going."

"I love you so much, you know that? You are the best cousin that a girl could ask for. You may be the only person in the world that I've said that to and meant it. I haven't even said it to Lucas yet."

"I love you more. Go on now. Get outta here. The people from everywhere gonna be looking for you soon."

"I know. Ok big cuz, I'm out. Catch you later."
Avionne gave her a tearful smile as she turned to
walk out the door. "Actually I probably won't."

Holding her son close in her arms, she bounded
down the stairs, looked around before exiting the
backdoor and blended in with the night.

Remi knew that this was her time. *I'm finally walking into my own.*

My Open Letter to You:

I finally realize that I have to grow up. I'm going to trust Nathan and see if he upholds his word. I'm going to raise Luna with as much Shia, Leigh and me I can get into her. I'm going to be more responsible and actually look like someone's mother. I'm saying goodbye to my colorful hair, my excessive piercings, and my tattoos. Ok the tattoos may be taking it too far, but I'll cover some of them up every now and then. I still have to be me you know.

The kids are great. Thanks for asking. ;) The twins are doing their thing. You know boys will be boys ... getting more into girls and being grown. Luna is resilient. She's bounced back the fastest and she will right the deaths in our family. I honestly think she's too young to really understand. She keeps the rest of us happy because she's happy and fearless. Truth be told, we could all learn a thing or two from her. She's the greatest kid on earth.

Vacation has been fun, but now it's time to return to the real world. I have to get them some stability. However, we are done with Greensboro. I do believe I am going to take them all back to Maryland where my siblings and I grew up. That place has always felt like home to me. I love everything about it. The sounds, the air, the way you can have city life in DC at night but be on your suburban tip by day.

I need to go back to where love was. My mom may have driven me crazy, but I loved her for what it's worth. It's ironic how my sister's parents and I were murdered by one of my mom's ex-lovers and Luna's parents were killed by her dad's ex-lovers daughter. History was repeating itself. I'm a do my best to break the cycle. These children and I will survive. We are survivors. Life has thrown us so many punches that it can't help but give us some sunshine. I know in my heart that there is a rainbow shining over a mountain somewhere with our names on it. And dog gon it I am going to find that mountain for us. I'm not saying I'm trying to be anyone's Mother Theresa, I don't plan on saving the world or anything, but please believe km going to save what's left of my family and that's just gonna be what it's gonna be.

Whether you like, love, hate me or have no opinion of me, know this ... it is finally Remi's turn to shine and I fully intend to do so. By any means necessary.

So be sure to tune into the next book by Mychea.

He Loves Me, He Loves You Not 5- Remi's story.

For the first time ever, it's all about me! :)

Till we meet again.

xoxo!

Remi

Email Mychea at: mychea@mychea.com

www.mychea.com

Books by Good2Go Authors on Our Bookshelf

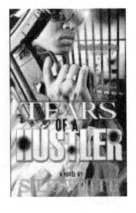

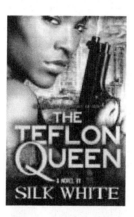

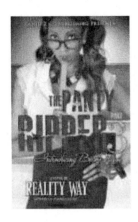

Good 2 Go Films Presents

THE HAND I WAS DEALT- FREE WEB SERIES

NOW AVAILABLE ON YOUTUBE!

YOUTUBE.COM/SILKWHITE212

To order books, please fill out the order form below:

To order films please go to www.good2gofilms.com

Name:_____

Address:_____

City: _____ State: _____ Zip Code: _____

Phone:_____

Email:_____

Method of Payment: Check   VISA   MASTERCARD

Credit Card#:_____

Name as it appears on card: _____

Signature: _____

Item Name	Price	Qty	Amount
48 Hours to Die – Silk White	$14.99		
Business Is Business – Silk White	$14.99		
Business Is Business 2 – Silk White	$14.99		
Flipping Numbers – Ernest Morris	$14.99		
Flipping Numbers 2 – Ernest Morris	$14.99		
He Loves Me, He Loves You Not - Mychea	$14.99		
He Loves Me, He Loves You Not 2 - Mychea	$14.99		
He Loves Me, He Loves You Not 3 - Mychea	$14.99		
He Loves Me, He Loves You Not 4 – Mychea	$14.99		
Married To Da Streets – Silk White	$14.99		
My Besties – Asia Hill	$14.99		
My Boyfriend's Wife - Mychea	$14.99		
Never Be The Same – Silk White	$14.99		
Stranded – Silk White	$14.99		
Slumped – Jason Brent	$14.99		
Tears of a Hustler - Silk White	$14.99		
Tears of a Hustler 2 - Silk White	$14.99		
Tears of a Hustler 3 - Silk White	$14.99		
Tears of a Hustler 4- Silk White	$14.99		
Tears of a Hustler 5 – Silk White	$14.99		
Tears of a Hustler 6 – Silk White	$14.99		
The Panty Ripper - Reality Way	$14.99		
The Panty Ripper 3 – Reality Way	$14.99		
The Teflon Queen – Silk White	$14.99		
The Teflon Queen 2 – Silk White	$14.99		
The Teflon Queen 3 – Silk White	$14.99		
The Teflon Queen 4 – Silk White	$14.99		

Time Is Money - Silk White	$14.99		
Young Goonz – Reality Way	$14.99		
Subtotal:			
Tax:			
Shipping (Free) U.S. Media Mail:			
Total:			

Make Checks Payable To:
Good2Go Publishing
7311 W Glass Lane,
Laveen, AZ 85339

CPSIA information can be obtained
at www.ICGtesting.com
Printed in the USA
LVOW04s2330061115

461517LV00017B/598/P

DEC 1 8 2015